Sowin' Seeds and Touchin' Lives

by

Carol A. Krejci, R.N.

DEDICATION

This book is lovingly dedicated to my God-given, Heartwarming friend, Stephanie Whitcraft.

Original illustrations within the book by Stephanie Whitcraft.

Special Literary Contribution by James F. LeSar, MD
Internal Medicine
Staff Member, Fairfield Medical Center
Lancaster, Ohio

"*Follow Me*"
Original Portrait by
Joyce Marion
Lancaster, Ohio

"To cry is to sow,"

said the maharal of Prague.

"To laugh is to reap,

and to write

is to sow and reap at the same time".

From:
"ALL RIVERS RUN TO THE SEA—MEMOIRS"
By Elie Wiesel, 1995

TABLE OF CONTENTS

FOREWORD

I met Carol Krejci, the author of this book, many years ago at a Hospital Christian Fellowship conference. Little did I know that this pretty, sweet smiling nurse with her warm and unassuming personality would go through a long and deep valley of pain and grief. Many of her closest friends as well as her parents passed away from deadly diseases within a brief span of time. The last one to leave her was her most precious friend, Stephanie Whitcraft, about whom this book is written.

Yet, this is a book about hope and life, about peace, purpose and joy. Through a long period of recovery from her losses, God has given Carol the opportunity to share Stephanie's tender heart and unselfish care toward her and others as they worked together - a most remarkable journey.

Through Carol, Stephanie's life has enriched mine and given it more meaning. Stephanie's unique way of reaching out and touching people's lives is something that will keep the reader spellbound - an example and inspiration to all of us.

I am also amazed at the details of Carol's carefully kept notes and journals that bring to life her times shared with Stephanie in these pages.

Carol and Stephanie's lives have deeply touched mine and given me courage and faith, together with them, to reach toward the goal of hearing Jesus' words one day: "Well done, my good and faithful servant."

Aubrey Beauchamp, R.N.
Founder, (1972) USA
Hospital Christian Fellowship, Inc.

PREFACE

The Question

The question had plagued my mind for most of my life, and it took long years of sorrow and losses to find the answer. It always has, and always will remain where it belongs with God alone. He has the answer and because He is sovereign, He does not have to give us any answers. Rather, He has trusted us with the unexplained.

Over forty years ago, at the age of fifteen, I absolutely could not understand that the loving God I believed in could allow my little neighbor boy to die of a lingering and painful battle with kidney cancer, but it happened. Later, during my nurse's training years, of course, I had to confront many unbelievable situations of devastating illness and overwhelming loss. We students were expected to avoid any close relationships with our patients and were subject to disciplinary action if we were observed to be non-compliant concerning this rule. Our instructors knew of the danger that could befall us — allowing our true compassion for our patients to overflow into our personal lives.

It was impossible to avoid these attachments completely, and as young women barely out of high school, we often mentally took our patients home with us at the end of the day, and frequently fell asleep with them on our minds. The instructor's job was to enable us to eventually function competently as professionals, never losing sight of our primary reason for choosing nursing as a profession - to care for the sick. This could easily be compromised if we allowed ourselves to become too closely involved with our patients.

The patient I came to love and embrace was named Linda who was only eleven years old. She was a beautiful little girl who had been admitted to the Pediatrics department with an extremely swollen and painful knee. She cried all the time. I chose Linda to be my patient for the assigned Case Study for the Pediatrics course. I was expected to follow Linda's case from the time of admission to her discharge, presenting all facets of her illness – symptoms, diagnosis, treatment and prognosis. The Case Study would also include information on her family unit, home environment, and religious and social life. Eventually all of the information would be compiled in a report (a term paper of sorts), and turned in to be graded.

I was Linda's student nurse for her entire hospital stay, and was with her five days a week for five weeks. An x-ray had shown a huge growth along the lower third of her femur. At surgery, a biopsy was performed which proved the lesion on her bone was malignant. The surgical treatment in 1960 was to remove the entire leg at the hip joint. This was performed immediately, and yet the outlook appeared grim.

"She may live another five months", the surgeon said.

I put my heart and soul into the care of this little girl, quickly drew very close to her family, and became consumed with thoughts about her and the battle ahead. She began to ask the evening and night shift nurses to "please call Nurse Carol", which, of course, they were not permitted to do. They would relay this to me the next morning, and my heart would ache with wanting to do more and more for her. Soon, I began to visit with her in the evenings, despite the rules.

The Search

One evening, as I approached her room, I heard her crying, and calling out to God.

"What did I do wrong? I'm sorry! Please forgive me! It hurts!

Please, God, what did I do wrong?"

My innocent nineteen-year-old heart began to cry out to Him, too. *"Indeed, Lord, what did a little eleven-year-old child do to deserve this? You are a kind and loving God, so why is this happening? Where are You?"*

There was no answer, so I kept on loving her trying to make it all better.

Within five months she was dead, and I found myself running to our Chaplain for answers. He had no answers for me, even tried to change the subject. He left me alone to cry out again and again, *"Where are You, Lord? Why did Linda have to suffer and die? I know it is within Your power to heal her, so why didn't You?"*

I was devastated by her death. Perhaps I never really got over the loss of this child, for I cried for days and days, and still cry to this day. I began to pray in earnest for my family members, *"Please, dear God, don't ever let anyone else I love die of cancer".*

I also began my own serious search for the God of the Bible, for He had not yet become a Friend of mine.

Over the next seventeen years, I searched for Him...in the Bible, in various church denominations, in science and in the writings of Josephus, the ancient Jewish historian. I knew He was there, I just had to find Him and know Him.

I found Him in March of 1978, on my knees in my parents' Pennsylvania home, the night before my father's surgery. He had a growth in his esophagus, most likely cancerous. *"Please, God, oh, please, please, don't let my Dad have cancer!"*

I cried until I had no more tears, and then I felt Him enclose me in His love! An invisible covering of warmth enveloped my whole being – body, spirit, and mind.

The warmth felt like a gentle blanket that conformed to my entire body. My spirit responded in awe that He would visit me in such a real way, and my mind was instantly at peace.

"How could this be?"

I had never made a full commitment to Him, and my search had led me in and out of churches, along with long periods of drought, not reading His Word or praying to Him. Yet, here I was, so undeserving, begging in my time of need…and He heard me!

He answered me! Psalm 40:1-2 explains how I felt.

> *I waited patiently for God to help me; then He listened and heard my cry. He lifted me out of the pit of despair; out from the bog and mire, and set my feet on a firm, hard path and steadied me as I walked along.*

Yes, He entered into my life in a new and wondrous way at a time when He seemed most distant.

He was there!

And He held me in His arms and let me cry.

My father did have cancer, and after a two-year battle, he died.

Within the next seven years, I would also lose my mother, and my two best friends to cancer and God never explained why. He was trusting me with the unexplained, and I, in turn, was learning to trust Him with the unexplained.

Oh, I cried, and asked 'why' so many times over those long years, yet no answer was to be found. Besides, no answer would have satisfied me for I was losing my loved ones. What I did know, however, was that we live in a fallen world where there is pain, suffering and sorrow.

I myself have had two failed marriages and was diagnosed with Bipolar Disorder, following a hospitalization for severe depression in 1990.

For fourteen years, the tears stopped. I felt as though I had stopped living. It was a dark time.

The Lord has never given me any explanation for any of it, but I do know this: I know that God is Love…totally, unconditionally, all-consuming, and ever-present.

Whether or not He answered any of my prayers for healing, be it physical or emotional, for others or myself, I know He was there.

I am so grateful that I recorded so many evidences of His presence in my life during those earlier years, for I did not write again for so many more. My journals during 1982 to 1987 are filled with praise reports, many of which came about because someone listened to God's 'nudges' to them on my behalf. Had they not heeded, the journals would not have been so full of wonders. Sorrow and loss are there as well, but His presence through it all shows that He cares in a most individual and profound way. I am writing again, and excited about recording His wondrous deeds once more, and am so grateful for the opportunity to share His goodness to me with others.

The Answer

Writing this book has been a journey back in time to those sad years, as I had to constantly refer to my journals for details and time frames. It has been painful, yet I knew I had to continue. I wanted to address this eternal question of 'Where is God?' and give evidence of His constant presence among us at all times and in all circumstances, even when it would appear that He is not there.

Another area of search I have not mentioned was in Nazi Germany. For years, I did not understand my deep interest in this darkest period of history. I never understood why I wanted to read everything I could get my hands on regarding this subject. I wondered why I would be so interested in the most unbelievably heinous acts of man's inhumanity to his fellow man.

As millions of others have asked, so did I. What would possess a nation to single out an entire culture of people to torture, starve, and murder by the millions, in an attempt to annihilate them without a backward glance. Granted, not all people were a part of this horror, but, for the most part, whether because of fear or allegiance to Hitler, a nation of cultured people listened to an insane dictator, and believed his lies that the oppressed ones were vermin to be destroyed and eliminated!

Every day, people like you and I were reduced to the depths of evil, and they appeared to do it willingly. There is no logic or answer except that man is sinful, and I believe Nazi Germany is a prime example of the depravity of which we are all capable. That is terrifying! God made us in His image, and yet individually we must choose which way we shall go.

After years of searching and reading, I began to wonder more about the faith of the Holocaust victims. Where did they get the strength to go on each day? Some were hiding in fear for months, even years, and often lived in subhuman conditions. In the concentration camps with the constant fear of the ovens, many lost their entire families to torture, starvation and slave labor. I wondered about their faith and began to read biographies of the survivors, all the while seeking answers to my own questions. I saw that just as we all react to life differently, so did they.

Many bravely joined the resistance and fought in an endless attempt to escape or assail their enemies. Many millions of others unbelievably kept putting one weak foot in front of the other, though barely able to function, until they could no longer go on. Some threw themselves against the electric wires of the concentration camps, finally escaping the horror in which they lived, and some continued the rituals of their faith with great risk to their lives.

But what about their faith?

Did they cry out to God *"Where are You?"* Did they denounce Him? In their despair, did they beg and plead as I did for my father's life? Did they shed billions of tears to a God who seemed to be absent? And was He really collecting all those tears in His bottle as the psalmist says,

You have seen me tossing and turning through the night.
You have collected all my tears and stored them in your

bottle! You have recorded every one in your book.

(Psalm 56:8)

How could a good and loving God be in this situation, in these places of evil, in this Hell? I wondered did they shake their fists into the air ladened with the ashes of their people, perhaps even their family members, to a God who couldn't possibly exist?

How would I have reacted to God had I been a Holocaust victim? It frightened me to even consider this question, for all too often during the years of loss in my life, I shouted to Him, *"Are You there, or are You and Your angels on vacation? We are all suffering down here on this little planet You created, or haven't You noticed?"*

Yes, I became angry, despairing, and wanted to die too, many times. *"No more, Lord, please"*, I sobbed. *"Send Jesus back and end this terror in which we all exist"*.

But instead of thunderbolts or striking me dead for my outbursts, He kept on showering me with His love. Despite it all, I could only continue to believe and pray, as He demonstrated His eternal presence time and again in the midst of the darkness of my life.

He was not absent at all.

He never goes on vacation, nor does He sleep, or turn a deaf ear to our pleas. He continues loving us with a love that is higher than the universe...there is no end! During their time in the concentration camps, Jews continued to call on the Eternal One, acknowledging His sovereignty.

It was during the time of reading the stories of the Holocaust survivors that I came to realize what God had been showing me all my life, and especially during the dark times. He continued to assure me of His eternal presence as I toured the Holocaust Memorial, Yad Vashem, in Jerusalem, as I prayed for my loved ones, and questioned the meaning of all the sorrow in the world.

It is this basic truth...that He is there in the midst of it all.

My search had finally culminated with an amazing insight as to His purpose for my life, and even as I struggled with my own faith during those times of sadness, He was planning to answer my helpless plea. *"Please, Lord, turn all of this into good, just as You promised. Give me beauty for ashes. Sorrow is lasting for this long night. I pray for joy in the morning. Please make it possible so that the deaths of my loved ones will not have been in vain"*, I pleaded. *"I will tell people of the many wonderful things You have done"*, I vowed.

It was then that He quietly whispered to my spirit,

"I ask that my Son's suffering not be in vain, Carol. He died for all of my loved ones. Tell them that".

It was then that I truly understood at last the mission He had given me.

God has graciously granted my request to tell others of the marvelous things He has done in my life and the lives of those I love. As you read this book, I pray you will only see His face, receive His love and continue to see Him in every aspect of your life, for He is there.

THE TRUST OF THE UNEXPLAINED

"I have been thinking of how many unexplained things there are in life. Our Lord Jesus who could have explained everything explained nothing. He said there would be tribulation but He never said why. Sometimes He spoke of suffering being to the glory of God but He never said how. All through the scriptures it is the same. I cannot recall a single explanation of trial, can you? We are trusted with the unexplained".*

*- Ruth Harms Calkin, 'Life's Little Prayer Book'

ACKNOWLEDGMENTS

God's incredible involvement from the original concept for this book to its completion is amazing and so I dedicate it to Him with gratefulness, and a prayer that those who read it will be drawn to a closer and more personal relationship with Him.

I will be forever grateful to God for bringing Stephanie Whitcraft, the original Heartwarmer, into my life.

To my children, Jim, Scott, Rob, and Laura, and my grandchildren Jennifer, Joshua, Stephany, David, Christian, Celena, Stacey, Justin, Haleigh, and Hannah who believed in this book and cheered me along the way.

A special message of thanks and love to the original Heartwarmer group members, Janet, Dolores, Wanda, and Amy and also to Pam, who brought me 'cookies in a doughnut box', and along with the cookies, a renewal of the vision for this book.

Thank you to Stephanie's daughters, Kathi Boyer and Tina Mason, for allowing me to pass on to others what each of us learned from being your mother's friend.

My deepest gratitude to my friend Dr. James LeSar for your devotion to serving the Lord in your medical practice and for going the extra mile time and again as you moved along the path God has laid before you. As you heed His guidance, you are where He wants you to be.

To Sara Thrash, Ph.D., who listened so closely to God, prayed for this book before I even knew about it, and thus confirmed my life's mission. May He bless you richly for your faithfulness and obedience.

To Aubrey Beauchamp, R.N., D.C., founder of the USA Hospital Christian Fellowship. Thank you for your encouraging and unfailing support of Stephanie's Heartwarmer ministry these past eighteen years, and for sharing with me your loving friendship, encouragement, skills, and knowledge. Thank you also for offering and performing the valuable task of typesetting this manuscript.

To my cousin, Susan Guerrieri, thank you for reading every chapter and helping me so much not only by your early editing, but also through your consistently encouraging comments and love.

A special thank you to a very special person, my Aunt 'Boots', who loved giving Heartwarmers to friends and fellow patients. Her belief in this book consistently sustained me, and I miss her so - she joined her loved ones with Jesus on March 6, 2004.

To my Aunt Jeanie, who gave me two of her precious Siamese kittens to love and fill my empty heart, I am so appreciative. I wish to express my gratitude also to my son Rob who drove to Pennsylvania to get the kittens and bring them home to me in Ohio. Within two short years, I had to give them up in order to make the move to San Diego. This was a dear price to pay as I loved them very much, but it was just not possible to bring them along.

To my son, Scott Hummel, thank you for recognizing your part in God's plan to bring me to beautiful San Diego, California, which was God's choice location for me to write this book. I offer my everlasting love and appreciation to you, Scott!

Last, but certainly not least, I want to express my love and gratitude to Julie Kirk, my special friend, mentor, and blessing from God, for your belief in the purpose of this book. Thank you, Julie, for urging me on and helping to make my feeble attempts to write this book become a reality. Thank you from the bottom of my heart for proofreading and editing the manuscript, but most of all, for your love. You are truly one of God's very special encouragers.

INTRODUCTION

This is the true story of God's very active presence in the lives of myself and those I love during times when it appeared God was absent. These were times filled with catastrophic illness and the courageous will needed to go on each day facing the unknown, because we know He is intimately in control of our lives and our circumstances.

Dedicating ourselves to the vision He has given each of us for our lives despite our circumstances here on earth can appear to be more than we possibly can do. Yet, the exciting part is to see and know that we are not going on our life's way alone. The One who gave us our purpose is going alongside us each step of the way. He has promised He would never leave us or forsake us, and we must believe this and act on this belief regardless of what is happening in our lives.

The person who by her life most exemplified this to me was my precious friend Stephanie Whitcraft, and her friendship was God's gift to me. Though He only gave us two years to know each other, we both believed He compacted a lifetime of friendship and learning into that short time frame. An elementary school teacher by profession, she was filled with exciting ideas and projects, but her greatest teaching assignment came to her from God, and I was privileged to be one of her students.

To allow someone to write her biography would not be her style. She was far too humble to allow that, and more importantly, she would want only God to be seen as the focus of any story about her life. This book does, however, reflect the life of a person who learned to give her all to the service of the Lord, despite a very personal loss and her own life-threatening illness.

When her husband Gary died in the fall of 1985, and she was told of her own recurring breast cancer, God gave her a specific work to do. But first, she had to learn that she must give up to Him not only the will to die, but also the will to live. If that seems contradictory, it really isn't, if we think about ourselves in the natural. Her husband was dead, she was about to enter her second course of chemotherapy in two years, and it was very frightening. She also had children - one daughter, Tina, sixteen years of age, still at home with her, and her older daughter, Kathi, who was recently married.

The will to die may have been a human need to be free of the acute sense of the loss of her husband, along with the fear of the unknown regarding her illness. The will to live, inherently within us by God's design, was most certainly focused on her desire to care for her children, for what emotion is stronger than the maternal?

But then, God gave her a dream of work she could do for Him here on earth, despite her situation. She had to determine to follow that dream wherever it would take her, and also to be willing to give up this work if and when He said her job on earth was finished. She chose to 'Follow Him', and the path He set before her. Many people, including myself, will never be the same.

It was during a difficult time in my life that God put Steph and I together, and at first I resisted, having already lost my father and a best friend to cancer. In the fall of 1985, I was taking care of my mother in my home. She was dying of cancer, and I had no strength for a relationship that would most likely result in another loss. Yet because of Steph's prayers, and my own feeble search for God's will in my life at the time, we were placed together as a team, for *'two are stronger than one.'*

> *Two can accomplish more than twice as much as one, for the results can be much better. If one falls, the*

> *other pulls him up; but if a man falls when he is alone,*
> *he is in trouble.*
>
> (Ecclesiastes 3:9-10)

We were both so weak yet, together in obedience, He made us strong.

This is the story of a friendship that was given only two short years, yet it is a marvelous story of what God can do if only we are willing to take the risks. God had much to say through Stephanie's ministry, and He placed me in a most strategic position - I was to go alongside Steph in order to enable her to travel and share His love in the unique way He had shown her.

I learned so much from my friend as she went along each day heeding the guidance of God's Holy Spirit and holding His hand. I felt compelled to write down in my journals the many wonderful things I was learning as we traveled and spoke to so many individuals during those two years. I have used the information from these journals to write this book, sharing examples of many documented occurrences as evidence of His loving care for us.

Her ministry began with little handmade cards of encouragement, which were called Heartwarmers. But He grew those Heartwarmers into something even more beautiful when she smiled and handed them to hurting people.

When she was first asked to share the story of the Heartwarmers (seeds of God's love for planting), she told me that God wanted me to go along with her at the same time to share my testimony. After our first public talk, we were invited to speak again and again, and people began referring to our sharing as a ministry. Stephanie's written testimony *"Sowin' Seeds and Touchin' Lives"* became the byline, if you will, of our combined Heartwarmer presentation.

Though He only allotted twenty-two months of time together, He made them rich and full, and we were blessed beyond words.

Shortly after pairing us together, He brought another beautiful person into our midst, a woman by the name of Amy Crook. A devoted Christian, she had met Stephanie and her husband Gary in her workplace as a Nuclear Technologist in the local hospital where we both worked. She was not only a beautiful person, but was blessed with a beautiful voice as well. When she offered to do anything to help with the ministry, we eagerly invited her to join us in our presentations and she accepted. She ministered in song and testimony – a perfect addition that only God could have achieved.

Despite illness, loss and grief, we were constantly able to see God's hand on our lives. "Where was God in all this?" some may ask. It is the overall theme and mission of this book to respond to this age-old question, as Stephanie did the last week of her life, *"He's here...in the trenches"*.

This book addresses the issue of where and when each of us enter these "trenches" as Christians, be it as family, friends or caregiver, and Who we bring along with us. God will place us where He wants us to be, as He wants to comfort His hurting children. We don't need to know the particulars, but just to follow the path He has laid before us, and He will bring them to us. We only need be obedient.

PART ONE

GETTING TO KNOW YOU

CHAPTER ONE

I'VE HEARD YOUR NAME BEFORE

As I look back now, I can see that 1984 was a most pivotal point in my life. At the time, I was miserably unhappy and lonely. A series of devastating events had turned my life upside down and all I could say was,

"Who am I and what am I doing here?"

I was working full-time as a visiting nurse and constantly felt like a fish out of water. My entire nursing career had been spent as a hospital nurse, and now I just couldn't find much purpose in my new job in home health. It had been a matter of necessity, this new job, as I had become an emotional wreck, and certainly not capable of performing my duties as a nursing supervisor. The stress of the job, along with the compounding effects of major losses in my life, was just more than I could bear.

"Please, Lord," I had prayed. *"Get me out of this. I just can't do it anymore."*

After eight years in the Emergency Room, I had been ready for a change. I started my job as a nursing supervisor in 1982 and was very excited to try a new avenue of my profession. I soon found out the challenges were far different, but I enjoyed them. My father had died of terminal cancer in 1980, and I felt I needed a change from the rigors and stresses of emergency nursing.

But, by the spring of the next year, 1983, my mother had developed very disturbing symptoms of muscle weakness. My brother had hurriedly brought her from Pennsylvania to my home in Ohio after we discovered she had only recently become unable to care for herself.

My own physician, Dr. James LeSar, had agreed to see her, and within a short period of time, had diagnosed her with a severe muscle weakness (polymyositis) secondary to the large breast tumor he discovered during his physical exam. As soon as possible surgery would be done. Hopefully, it would remove the cancer, and thus alleviate the symptoms of the polymyositis.

Unbelievably, she was admitted to the hospital room in which my dearest friend, Charlotte, lay a victim of terminal leukemia! A bone marrow transplant was Charlotte's only hope now, and she was transferred to OSU Hospital the day my mother went to surgery for her mastectomy.

My personal life was in shambles also, and within a few months, I would be divorced. I made the decision to move closer to my job, and to my mother's doctor for her chemotherapy treatments. But, the move also meant I had to leave my sixteen-year-old son Rob behind, as he had chosen to live with his father. This further broke my already breaking heart.

During the following year, my mother received her chemotherapy treatments, and also had two emergency operations, which led to lengthy stays in our Intensive Care unit. Somehow, we made it through the year and my mother, gratefully in remission, decided to return to Pennsylvania and her own home. It turned out to be a wonderful year as she gardened, traveled, visited with friends, and enjoyed her renewed health and strength.

A year later, almost to the day, she drove to Ohio for Easter, and we discovered the muscle weakness returning. This signified a more ominous concern – the return of the cancer. A visit to the doctor and subsequent scans confirmed our fears. It had indeed returned, and chemotherapy was started again.

My mother never was able to return to Pennsylvania again, except to sell the house she and Dad had built just a few years earlier. She stayed with my daughter and I until she died nine months later. It was a rough year, and I struggled to keep up with my job and home responsibilities.

Eventually defeated, I asked God to please get me out of the job situation as a hospital supervisor, as I knew I was no longer able to cope with stress.

Just when I thought I would break, circumstances occurred which allowed me to leave the hospital and be on staff with the Visiting Nurse Association, all within forty-eight hours!!

This was practically unheard of in the professional world, which ordinarily would have required two weeks to a month's notice to fill my position. I was so grateful to be set free, and gingerly stepped into uncharted waters.

It wasn't long, however, before I began to complain.

"What am I doing here? This isn't nursing. I want to go back to my hospital job!" (very reminiscent of the Israelites shortly after God had delivered them from Egypt).

But God knew what He was doing, as He tenderly introduced me to some very special people – people who would influence the rest of my life.

Janet was the first special person God put in my life. She was a Registered Nurse with the Visiting Nurses Association (VNA), and had been assigned to orient me to the process of visiting and assessing patients in their homes. We smile a little now as we look back on our first day 'in the field'. As we sat in her car, munching on our lunch, we shared a bit about ourselves, and both ended up crying our eyes out. *My* mother was dying of cancer, and *her* mother had just recently passed away from lung cancer. As we comforted each other, we also shared our faith in God, His love and His promises. Then and there, a friendship was born.

The next wonderful person I was to meet was Dolores, a tiny little lady, severely handicapped with rheumatoid arthritis. During my first visit to her home, I noticed a small plaque on the wall. It was a child cupped in God's hands.

> *See, I have tattooed your name upon my palm.*
> (Isaiah 49:16)

My mention of the plaque prompted Dolores to tell me how she applied this verse to her life.

"At night when I go to bed," she said, "I have this special little pillow. Into the center of that pillow goes my thumb. That thumb represents me and the pillow is God's hand. I go to sleep in the palm of His hand and that way I can rest."

Knowing that she was a Christian opened the door for us to share our faith. I excitedly told her about Hospital Christian Fellowship, (HCF) the medical organization to which I belonged, and ran out to my car to retrieve a copy of HCF's magazine, *A New Heart*. Dolores was so thrilled to know there was a medical organization with a mission of sharing Christ with patients and co-workers. It had been a physician who told her how much Jesus loved her when as a child, unable to walk, she had spent much time at Children's Hospital.

Though severely handicapped as an adult, using crutches, Dolores lived alone, and was actively involved in her church. Despite joints with limited movement, God had blessed her with nimble fingers enabling her to play the piano, and learn the skill of dressmaking and textile reweaving. She also had lots of little neighborhood children in and out of her home all the time. They always learned something about Jesus during their visits with her. Dolores was a dedicated Bible student and prayer warrior too. In fact, she became my spiritual nurse, and I was, in turn, her physical nurse. What a picture of the faithful, trusting servant of God she was!

During my first exciting visit to her home as I told her about HCF, she said,

"I have a friend you just have to meet. She will be thrilled to know about your organization".

The friend she wanted to introduce me to was an elementary school teacher, now on disability and fighting breast cancer. I shuddered as I thought of my mother, and her own battle with the same illness.

"Her name is Stephanie Whitcraft and you two have just got to meet!"

"Stephanie Whitcraft," I thought to myself. "I've heard that name before - but where? When?"

It was weeks later, after I learned from Dolores about Steph's card ministry, that it came to me.

"Oh! I know who told me about this person. It was Isabelle, my former co-worker at the hospital!"

Isabelle was the dayshift-nursing supervisor, and I had been a part time evening supervisor.

One day, during report, she mentioned to me that if I knew of anyone who needed cheering up, she could pass the information along to a former teacher she knew who had a card ministry to the sick and downhearted.

"Her name is Stephanie Whitcraft", Isabelle told me. "She taught my sons in elementary school".

As I recalled the talk with Isabelle, I also remembered that I had become intrigued with this person, Stephanie, someone who, though sick herself, wanted to reach out to others.

A fascinating chain of events had begun, and it would result in an experience and relationship only God could have produced.

CHAPTER TWO

DOUGHNUTS AND
RAINBOW MUGS

It's Saturday morning and I can sleep in today! It was a fleet-ing reminder that popped up in the midst of a dream, and in the twilight of my sleep. I smiled as I rolled over, rearranged my pillow, pulled the sheet over my head, and decided to resume my dream. Sometimes we can do that - continue our dreams, I mean, and other times it is just plain impossible when we drift back into our reverie and become aware of morning sounds such as the morning traffic or birds beginning their cheerful concerts. Children are laughing somewhere, or perhaps the phone rings. Something interrupts the process, and we really do wake up!

In my case, this Saturday morning, it was the barely percepti-ble sound of someone at my front door. Not a knock, not a doorbell ring, but somehow my subconscious mind detected that someone was at the door downstairs.

O.K., I said to myself. I'll let my curiosity get the best of me!

Reluctantly, I threw on my bathrobe, padded my way downstairs, turned on the coffee pot I'd filled the night before, and opened the front door. No one was there! No car in the driveway either! I looked down, hoping to see the Saturday newspaper, but instead, greeting me was a box from the local doughnut shop. Taped onto the box was a little card. *'Flowers For My Friend'*, it said.

The word *my* had been crossed out and in its place was the word *our.* Therefore it read, *'Flowers For Our Friend.'* I suspected this early morning treat was from my new 'telephone' friend, Stephanie Whitcraft, whom I had met through Dolores. There was no signature, but somehow I knew who it was from, though, at this point in time, I had never seen a Heartwarmer card.

Some weeks later, as I was driving home from work, the thought occurred to me that I could send something anonymously back to Steph and Gary. I felt that God was in on this little surprise, so I went with my first instinct – flowers for my friends whom I had yet to meet face to face.

In the floral shop, I spotted the perfect gift almost immediately. It was a small bouquet of flowers in a ceramic mug, which was decorated with a rainbow and clouds. I knew it was the right gift to send. Rather than a signature, I wrote on the gift card, *God loves you and so do I.*

Over the weeks, cards and calls between us increased, yet no mention was ever made of the doughnuts or the rainbow mug bouquet. We all were happily keeping our little secrets, or so we thought.

"Thank you for the flowers", she whispered softly, as I gave Steph a hug.

It was October 6th, 1985, and I had come to the funeral home to pay my respects to her husband Gary who had passed away. By then, Steph, Gary and I had met face to face only twice but they had both become increasingly dear to my heart.

She knew all along, I thought, and when I replied,

"And thank you for the doughnuts," a connection was made.

Later, she was to tell me how happy she was that Gary was still well enough at the time to enjoy the flowers.

Obeying these little 'nudges' we receive from God are the key to His special deliveries of love and reassurance, letting us know that He is there with us as we go through the troubled waters of this earthly life.

That is what is behind the special ministry of the Heartwarmers. By our obedience and by sowing these seeds, He can reach out and touch His hurting children. Steph explained it this way:

"Giving out Heartwarmers is God's way of showing me how to touch other people for Him, and also His way of helping me to cope with my own illness".

Steph's word's remind us that:

"God wants people to see Jesus in us".

Perhaps you have been the recipient of His love in such a manner, or perhaps you have acted on a tiny tug at your spirit and reached out to someone who was hurting. And has it not been an exciting adventure to be either the giver or the recipient of His goodness?

For more than four years rainbows had represented just that to me. That's why I sent the rainbow bouquet to Gary and Steph.

I'd like to tell you the story of my "Rainbow Lady", and how her consistent obedience to His promptings carried me through years of sorrow and loss.

SHOWERS OF BLESSINGS

The first card came just two days after I wrote the poem—the poem God had awakened me to write. Five o'clock in the morning has never been my time of day. I'm a night owl and much prefer the quiet and solitude of midnight. But that morning I awakened without the usual drowsiness, and with a cup of coffee as my companion and God as my inspiration, I wrote the poem.

A few weeks earlier, I had taken a plane trip to California, and the sight of a faint rainbow in the sky had encouraged me when I became anxious about the rainy weather. Now, it seemed He wanted me to tell others about this experience.

Just two days later, I received an unsigned card - a simple picture of clouds in a blue sky with a rainbow and the promising words:

Whenever clouds fill your sky,
remember God has a rainbow standing by.

Only three persons including myself knew about my poem at that time, and as much as I tried, neither of the others would admit to sending the card.

Two weeks later, another card arrived, again without a signature, but with a message of God's love, and the assurance of His constant and personal care for me.

At the time, I was having personal problems, and was overwhelmed that God cared enough to send me these cards. I knew they were from Him - but who was being His instrument in this? I wanted to know who listened so unquestionably, and sent cards so appropriately on His behalf.

It wasn't for me to know, but over a period of twenty-seven months, the rainbows kept coming, along with many thoughtful little gifts. During those longs months, I had many problems to deal with, and there were many times I almost gave up. But the realization of the cards, which, to my amazement, always came at the right time, kept my eyes on my Source of strength. He knew my needs, and He never failed me.

I am so thankful that person was obedient. By the time the rainbows stopped coming, just about all my earthly props had been taken from me, and I felt weak as a kitten. But, as each one was taken away, He was teaching me to lean more and more on Him. I didn't even realize until later the fullness of what had happened.

But now I am a much stronger person, not because I am any less sensitive to pain and losses, but because I know what He did in my life and how He renewed my strength. Now my strength is in Him and in Him alone. I count on His promises, for His word is true:

> _There is utter truth in all your laws: your decrees are eternal._
>
> (Psalm 119:160)

I can look to the Light through eyes clouded with tears, and still see the rainbow, for it was there all the time.

THE RAINBOW

The sky was misty as upwards we flew
"But above all those clouds," I was told, "the sky's blue."
And blue it became as the airplane flew high,
And we were enthralled with God's glorious sky.
Billows of white, fluffy clouds below, and blue for a canopy,
Truly a show of God's handiwork here in the air.
So we watched and enjoyed it with hardly a care.

But then it got grey, and it sprinkled some rain,
The weather got rough and we bounced in the plane.
"Oh, where are those blue skies," I thought, "I'm afraid."
The rain hit the window, the big airplane swayed.
"But look!" someone said, "just look over there"…
"A rainbow to look at! God truly does care!"

Yes, He sent us a rainbow as onward we flew
Across this vast country, in deep skies of blue.
Now, rain and grey skies came, where blue might have been,
But without them, the rainbow could not have been seen.
So is it in life, blue skies come and they go,

But just look through the rain for God's gift –
THE RAINBOW!

July, 1981

The cards continued to come until Christmas of 1983. During that time, many people were blessed and watched in amazement at God's perfect timing and beautiful expressions of love.

How we thank you, Lord! Your mighty miracles give proof that you care.

(Psalm 75:1)

I believe the challenge presented to all of us, myself included, is to pray for the awareness of God's still, small voice, and for the willingness to follow His leading. Whether we are going about our busy days, home alone or sick in body or spirit, we need to remind ourselves that He is the Master of time and space, and if we are but willing and obedient, He will use us again and again as He sends His "Showers of Blessings". Remember that showers fall not just on one person, but also on many others around us as we share with them what God can do.

CHAPTER THREE

SOWING SEEDS IN TEARS

Those who sow tears shall reap joy. Yes, they go out weeping, carrying seed for sowing, and return singing, carrying their sheaves.

(Psalm 126:5-6)

It was October 17th, the day before Laura's eleventh birthday. My mother lay terminally ill in our dining room turned hospital room. She couldn't be left alone, and as I thought about Laura's birthday, it seemed improbable that I would be able to do much for her this year. I needed to go shopping to buy gifts, a cake mix and ice cream.

It was a beautiful fall day, yet overwhelming sadness engulfed me. Every time I went into the kitchen in our small townhouse, I was exposed to the sorrowful sight of my mother lying in her hospital bed, sleeping or staring at the wall.

We had tried to make her room as homey as possible, adding a couple pieces of her own familiar furniture, along with some favorite pictures on the walls near her bed of her children and

grandchildren. There was a double-hung window with gauze cur-
tains that allowed plenty of glowing sunshine into her room to
brighten her days and at the same time helped to keep her warm.
She was weak and always so cold.

This existence was a far cry from her lovely home in
Pennsylvania, with its five acres of beautifully kept lawns. Fruit
and vegetable gardens surrounded the brick, ranch-style house
she and Dad had built before their illnesses had so brutally inter-
rupted their lives.

As long as Mom was able, she spent a lot of time at the farm
with my brother, Alec, and his wife, Lois. She loved being in the
country, and she had a renewed sense of purpose whether by helping with cooking, cleaning, or "putting up" the harvest from my
brother's garden. She loved being there so much!

What must it be like, I wondered, to have had all of that, and
now be a prisoner of this cancer and its accompanying and relent-
lessly progressive muscle paralysis? I was unable to comprehend
the impact of all of this, though I longed to be able to understand,
help, and somehow make it better.

Now, here she lay, totally dependent on others, alone with her
thoughts and fears. Laura and I were her only caregivers at this
point in time, and at her tender age, Laura was a precious granddaughter and had assumed the role of a wonderfully compassionate "nursing assistant", a role which she performed faithfully and
lovingly. She never complained about the fact that having her
friends over might disturb her grandmother.

And now, on the eve of her birthday, I wanted so much for her
to have a happy and special day. I hadn't yet figured out how to
leave the house to do the shopping for her cake and birthday gifts.

Then the phone rang, and as I picked it up and said hello, the
soft, sweet voice of Stephanie responded.

"Hi," she said. "I was wondering if you'd like to get out of
the house this afternoon? I will come and stay with your mother".

My mind was whirling. What kind of person is this Stephanie? I asked myself. After all, she was still in mourning, as Gary had just died two weeks before...to the day! She herself had just started a second round of chemotherapy for recurrent breast cancer, and yet, she had called and offered herself and her afternoon to stay with someone terminally ill with the same illness she was fighting. We talked a bit, and eventually I reluctantly agreed to accept her offer. Months later, as we discussed this, she told me that God had told her to call me that day.

Steph had no idea of my need to shop for Laura that day, but she had acted on the 'nudge' she had received from God. It wasn't long before she was knocking at my door. I did my shopping and was home within a couple of hours, happy with my purchases and grateful to my new friend. It was a wonderful reprieve for me to be able to do this. Steph met me at the door and quietly said,

"Your mother never talked the whole time you were gone, but that's O.K. I just sat in the living room and read."

I laid down my packages and peeked in on my sleeping mother. Then Steph and I went outside in the warm sun and talked. We hadn't had a personal sharing time before this, but she had been calling and sending cards to Laura, my mother, and myself. In fact, by this time, I had only talked with her face to face two other times since our first phone conversation in June. This day, October 17, 1985, as we shared our sorrows and faith, our friendship was sealed. As we prayed together, we sensed a special bond developing, and also an awareness that God's hand was definitely on this friendship.

Weeks later, as we talked about her ministry, the words of the Psalmist opened up to us.

Those who sow tears shall reap joy.

(Psalm 126:5)

We agreed with the Psalmist's words, and weeks later, as we developed her written testimony, *Sowin' Seeds and Touchin' Lives*, we knew for a certainty that by reaching out and touching lives in God's Name, though in sorrow ourselves, He would allow us to reap joy, regardless of our circumstances.

We had no idea just how true those words would be in our lives, but God does honor His Word. He definitely keeps His promises, of that we can be sure! Psalm 146 tells us,

> *He is the God who keeps every promise.*
>
> (Psalm 146:6)

What more do we need to know?

"Keep on sowing your seed . . .

CHAPTER FOUR

CLOWNING AROUND

Have you ever wanted to meet a clown? Better yet, have you ever wanted to *be* a clown? During the month of November 1985, after Gary had died, I learned just how much Stephanie wanted to be a clown...a silent clown for God, that is.

She told me she was waiting for an assignment and that she knew she would be visiting hospitals and nursing homes someday. She was so sure of this that she had already made the clown outfit. She also told me that God had planned its design.

It didn't seem too much to ask of Him, she had said, if only He would just arrange a few assignments for her. Of course, she knew He could do that anytime, and so she waited eagerly.

This is how it finally happened.

Early in November, she had gone to her doctor about a lump she found on the site of her previous mastectomy. She was frightened, as we all were, and her name was in our constant prayers.

At my home, my mother was steadily deteriorating and extremely weak following a late September hospitalization for bacterial meningitis.

I had just resigned from my Home Health job, and had been rehired at my hospital to work in the Emergency Room two nights a week, as I would now be caring for my mother even more than before.

Steph and I had developed a friendship, mostly by telephone, and it was on the phone that I heard from her concerning the biopsy report. The suspicious lump was malignant, and the cancer was already in both her lungs and ribs. It was during this conversation that she offered me a chance to 'bow out gracefully', since I'd already lost one friend to cancer. I was dumbfounded by this comment and was having a hard time understanding God's allowance. Gary had just died, and Steph had a sixteen-year-old daughter to raise. I found myself reminding God of this fact as I asked Him to heal her, yet knowing I must acknowledge His sovereignty. Amazingly, she had actually gone to visit a cancer patient at the hospital that very same day!

We had been spending a lot of time on the phone during those days, and I was finding that her honesty about her health was also causing me to confront its reality. I was so afraid as we were fast becoming friends.

Within a few days, she started her chemotherapy regime, yet she asked us to have our Bible study at her house. This all seemed so incredible to me, and we were all a little overwhelmed.

I wasn't ready for this!

It was really beginning to hurt!

Going to her house also meant leaving my mother with someone else, and then, of course, returning and facing yet another illness – my mother's.

My dear friend Charlotte and Mom had been roommates in our hospital, and I remembered the emotional tug-of-war that had been waged within me during that time. I had long before promised Charlotte I'd be there for her, and that even if no one else could let her talk freely about her fears, I would.

Of course, I never expected that she and my mother would become roommates, as she faced her final bout with leukemia, and my mother began her battle with breast cancer.

I remember standing between the two beds, overwhelmed with grief as I tried to be daughter, friend and nurse. There are no words to describe how I felt. I could see that I was becoming very familiar with Isaiah 53:3 as he describes the Messiah—

...a man of sorrows, acquainted with bitterest grief.
(Isaiah 53:3)

I was comforted by the knowledge that He understood—because He had been there!

Now, it seemed I was going to be dealing with the same thing again. There was just no way that I could not be Steph's friend, and so I gave it all up to God to work out. The night before she was to start chemotherapy, she called to be sure that I would understand if she wasn't up to talking when I called to check on her. Imagine that!

The next day, my mother's temperature was up, and Laura was home sick, but upon checking on Steph that evening, I was grateful to learn she'd had a fairly good first day.

The following Monday, we were invited to have our Bible study at Steph's house. It would allow her to be a part of it, yet be comfortable in her own home. We all agreed. I made arrangements for my mother and Laura's care, and we headed to Steph's house where Dolores would lead the Bible study.

We were met at the door by an adorable white-faced clown with a big, wide smile and a shiny red heart sticker on her right cheek! Stephanie was totally irresistible as she smiled and without a word, handed each of us a Heartwarmer.

Her clown outfit was divided down the middle from top to bottom, one side was white, and the other side red. Big patchwork pockets of the opposite side's material made lots of room for the little cards (pockets full of joy!). A white jester's collar with little jingle bells at the tips, and a duster's cap completed the outfit.

She told us later that God had given her the complete design for the costume, including the colors and material, and she now was eager to put it to use. When she finally did go on her first 'assignment', she brought along her companion, a fluffy bunny, complete with its own outfit matching hers.

But that comes later, and I'll remember to tell you.

One evening, shortly after she had begun her chemotherapy, Steph and I were able to go out for dinner. It was a very special time of sharing. She talked freely about her illness and treatment, and her desire to serve the Lord despite her health. She prayed that her illness 'might serve Him'. This was a part of one of her favorite prayers, entitled, *I Have My Mission*, by John Henry Cardinal Newman.

Steph told me of her yearning to go into hospitals and nursing homes as a silent clown for God, and that she wanted an 'assignment' so badly.

As we talked over dinner, I (the nurse) reminded her that perhaps it wasn't yet the right time. Tears filled her eyes, as she acknowledged the effects a new chemotherapy regime could have on her. God collected those tears and He stored them in His bottle just as it says in Psalm 56:8,

> *You have collected all my tears and preserved them in your bottle!*

Only God knew the impact His little clown was to have in the future on hundreds of hurting people. The Lord was planning something beautiful and His clown was to be His unique instrument of healing. But it wasn't yet the right time. So she bloomed where she was planted, and continued to draw and color the little Heartwarmers, visiting cancer patients (including my own mother), and waited on Him.

When she was at last able to visit a nursing home, she showed up at my door, all dressed and ready to go! The picture I took of the smiling clown with Bunny, her companion, that morning is priceless.

Her companion had a friend, which was also a bunny. He arrived at my home one day, all wrapped up in a box, as a gift for my mother. The sticker on the box said it was for Ann from Stephanie with love. The directions were as follows:

Take me out of the box and hug me - even maybe I could sleep with ya... Please? I'm little, who would know?

Dear Ann, Please squeeze me and shhh...put me under or on your pillow where I can keep ya warm and love ya, O.K? I represent God's peace and love.

Love,
The Bunny

And do you know what my mother did with the bunny who "represented" God's love? She held it close to her under the covers.

How did Steph know what to write on the package? Do you think she knew what my mother's response to the bunny would be? I believe she simply listened to the nudge she received from God, and acted upon it. He knew exactly how my mother would react, and it was His pleasure to use Steph to bring a special delivery of His love to her.

So often, we do nothing for fear of a person's response to our offer, but as the last line of one of Steph's poem reminds us,

May my little, as the widow's mite,
be accepted - as just right!

He is the Giver, and if we act on His promptings, how can we go wrong? If we allow our human fears to get in the way, the blessing cannot take place. It may have seemed like a little thing, but it reached into my mother's heart. Even today, as I write this, it is reaching into other's hearts and souls, of that I am sure.

PART TWO

A HEARTWARMING MINISTRY

CHAPTER FIVE

CHOOSE LIFE

March 7, 1986. It was my mother's birthday, and there I was with Steph standing in front of a group of one hundred women in the First United Methodist Church in our hometown. It was the World Day of Prayer, and we were about to share our prayerfully considered combined testimonies for the first time.

Three weeks prior, and only two weeks after my Mother had passed away, I had introduced Steph to the staff of the Visiting Nurses at their request. By that time, they had heard so much about this gentle woman and her Heartwarmer cards that the administrator asked for a presentation - an in-service about sharing and caring.

These same nurses and nursing assistants, my co-workers, included those who had just recently helped care for my mother. Although I saw that my contribution was to introduce Steph, she felt I was to have more to say — a brief testimony.

"O.K.," I thought, "I can do that. I can't turn down an opportunity to witness to this group of health care workers. I promised Him I would tell others what He had done for me whenever and wherever possible."

My friends were deeply moved by what they heard that day, as Steph told the story behind the Heartwarmers. She also shared her thoughts on the difference a small gesture can make in a patient's life, reassuring the busy staff that even if they only had time to fluff a pillow or touch a grieving family member on the shoulder, they could be touching for God, and He will do the rest. The message was simply this — God really does want to enter into these circumstances filled with pain, sorrow, fear, or illness, and He does that through all of us, His servants. It gave the frequently overworked staff reason to believe that they could positively affect the lives of not just their patients, but their families as well.

Two weeks later, Steph was invited to speak to the women's group for the World Day of Prayer, and she was insisting that God wanted me to go with her to speak to them. I struggled against this, for I had recognized her truly unique testimony, and wondered just what I could add, as hers seemed so complete. What would I have to say?

I listened to Steph's reasoning.

"It's what God wants," she had said.

So I prayed.

In time, He assured me that I was to go with Steph, and reminded me that I was to tell others what He had done for me and not what I had done for Him. I eventually concluded that if God had linked us together, then I must stop questioning Him and simply be obedient.

The theme for the World Day of Prayer, *CHOOSE LIFE,* was a real test of our faith in God's enabling power, as we prayed and discussed the things we would be talking about — the illnesses and deaths that had entered our lives. We were still grieving the losses of our loved ones, and also Steph's diagnosis of recurrent cancer.

"He's got us right on the pain line, Carol," Steph was to say.

Yes, He certainly did, and because of that, we had to be carried by the Holy Spirit, the Comforter, the Enabler, and the God of all compassion. Sharing with others the substance of our broken hearts, yet buoyed by the excitement of serving the Lord, we simply were able to say,

> *Not by might, nor by power, but by my Spirit, says the Lord of Hosts—you will succeed because of my Spirit, though you are few and weak.*
> (Zechariah 4:6)

We were broken and poured out, and that was where He wanted us to be, on the 'pain line'. Then, and only then, He was able to minister to others in His own special way, as He filled these empty vessels to overflowing.

Impossible?

In the natural, yes, perhaps it would be impossible. We were to talk about choosing life, yet we would be sharing with others our most recent losses, along with our individual fears and weaknesses. But the message was clear: CHOOSE LIFE! Choose today which way you shall go.

Painful?

Oh, yes.

Frightening?

Absolutely, for after all, we did not know what lay ahead or how we would respond to these emotionally painful disclosures.

It seemed impossible, but we were entering into God's work, and would therefore be totally dependent on His awesome power to overcome all of these earthly concerns. He had made no 'new' promises, but we counted on and claimed His every promise as we prepared to follow Him in this endeavor.

We had no idea that this very emptying was to be repeated innumerable times over the next two years, but He walked ahead of us, step by step, allowing us time to stop and rest our spirits. So we chose life as we spoke that day, cried a little and never looked back.

I'm wondering if He has given you a special direction for your life. I would like to reassure you that this would be a thrilling adventure if you turn all the particulars over to Him.

Don't worry about how or when or where, for His plan is perfectly fitted for you, and you alone. He knows what He is doing and never makes mistakes. Be available, give Him all of yourself and simply say like Isaiah,

> *"Then I heard the Lord asking, 'Whom shall I send as a messenger to my people? Who will go?' And I said, "Lord, I'll go. Send me!"*

(Isaiah 6:8)

CHAPTER SIX

 ## SHARING HERE AND THERE

In record time, Steph and I became not only fast friends, but increasingly committed to working together for God's purposes. At first, we simply enjoyed being together, alone or with our daughters, just to talk, bake, eat, and get to know each other better. In December, we busied ourselves making Christmas cookies with the girls and concentrating on the reason for Christmas. With Steph only recently being widowed and me caring for my mother, keeping our eyes on Him, the precious Baby, and His reasons for coming to earth, allowed us to face the bleak days of winter with hope.

Things really began to pick up though after the holidays. Ideas were developing in Steph's mind at practically lightening speed, and I was simply riding along on her coattails, so to speak.

The entire month of January, 1986 was filled with a schedule that would exhaust a healthy person, let alone the two of us!

Caring for my mother was very intense during this, the last month of her life, but nevertheless God energized us with excitement and challenges.

Our first project together grew from our mutual desire to develop a support group for cancer patients and their families. We discussed this with a few interested professionals and had numerous planning meetings to discuss our goals and hopes for this group. All of this planning took place during the winter weeks before my mother passed away. In fact, our last planning session was held the day before she died. By then, we had obtained permission from the local American Cancer Society to meet in their building once a month, had determined our meeting schedule, and obtained our mailing database. Steph drew the logo for 'The Circle of Hope', as we named it, and the very next week postcards were sent to prospective members.

Our first meeting, held in February, had thirteen people in attendance. and was very well-received. The group is still an active and respected organization in Lancaster.

Steph had mentioned to me that she had a desire to put together a small booklet of encouraging ideas to help people cope with overwhelming illnesses such as her own. She talked about me writing a booklet of encouragement for caregivers because I was a nurse and had been keeping my experiences as a Christian in the medical field, including caring for my parents, in my journals.

I had shared some of the experiences from my journals with her, as God's interventions were so exciting and mind- boggling, and I liked sharing them.

Steph suggested,

"Since your stories are already written, you should not keep them in a notebook, but share them with others as they will give hope to the readers".

She knew her booklet would consist of fewer words, and more hand-drawn pictures, as this would be easier to read, not requiring a lot of time, energy, or concentration.

"In other words", she said, "You write stories, Carol, and I will write thoughts".

She offered to draw the accompanying pictures for each booklet, and also the cover drawings. We spent hours on the phone and at each other's homes putting our booklets together, covering each aspect in prayer.

Before I know it, we were at the print shop where her Heartwarmers were produced, discussing our booklets with the owner. As reality set in, we became increasingly enthused with this project.

Since I was still caring for my mother, our frequent late-hour telephone conversations were a must, but they produced exciting results.

Before we even spoke at the women's World Day of Prayer, we had been invited by one of the VNA staff members to speak at her church. There were also three other possible dates for the future that day, along with a monetary donation toward the Heartwarmer ministry, a term that was totally new and awesome to us. It seemed a tall order to fill, and was equally intimidating. We were already hard at work on our meditation booklets, and busy with our individual lives. We were both raising our daughters alone, and Steph was dealing with chemotherapy too while I was working three nights a week in the Emergency Room. We did not dismiss our grief in any way, but kept on going in spite of it.

The work on the booklets, designed to be an encouragement to patients (Steph's booklet) and the healthcare giver (my booklet) took a lot of time but they were complete and ready to be printed within three months time.

We found ourselves exceptionally busy and to get away from it all, we had begun a tradition by going out to eat every other Saturday night. After a few of these relaxing evenings, we decided to continue doing this no matter how busy we became.

It was during those wonderful times together that we shared so many ideas, plans, and tears. In fact, tears of joy and sorrow flowed freely during those precious hours away from everything else in our lives. I was learning to listen closely as she talked not only about her fears and anxieties, but more importantly, all the 'neat things' God was doing in her life. She was so exciting to be with that I often had to remind myself that she was sick. I never wanted to lose sight of that or ever take her for granted. I prayed that she would always feel free to talk with me about anything she needed to share, and that I would be able to be honest in expressing my feelings of inadequacy and insecurity regarding our relationship. I believe her prayer was very similar to my own — and I know that God responded.

We had a fantastic friendship, both in the natural as well as spiritually, that lasted through countless lunches and dinners until the end of her life. We *never* ran out of things to talk about, and sharing excitedly what God was doing in our lives, both individually and as a team, was the most thrilling of all. Our journals, which we kept as faithfully as possible, often paralleled each other, and this left us even more amazed at God's ability to individualize His touch on our lives. The journals changed day-by-day, as God kept adding to our dreams and fulfilling them.

The consistency of our 'dinners out' was an unexpected source of comfort to us, and this simply added to the dimension of our friendship. When she became too ill and weak to continue this custom, we simply 'ate in'. We'd agree on a favorite restaurant, and I would bring the food to her home, enabling us to continue our special times together during those most difficult days.

During the early weeks and months of 1986, the invitations for Steph and I to speak seemed to mushroom. The Heartwarmer ministry was indeed reaching the hearts of others, and as far as I can remember, people heard about what we had to say simply by word of mouth, or an occasional newspaper article written by someone. Never once in two years did we promote anything except God, for this is what He had ordained.

Each time, before we spoke to any group, we needed to be lifted up in prayer, as our subject was always regarding bringing God's presence into difficult situations of loss, fear and grief. The only examples we used were from our own lives. That meant discussing the most painful things that had ever happened to us. We told these same stories not once, not twice, but *every* time we stood up to speak to a group, and we coveted the prayers of our friends and listeners. We were always careful to say that we knew everyone suffered pain and loss, and did not want it to seem as though we felt we had 'cornered the market' on pain (Steph's suggestion). I think God had given her keen insight in that regard, and we prayed each time before we spoke that we not forget to relate this to our audience.

One speaking engagement led to another, and we were constantly overwhelmed at what God was doing. We had been spending so much time together collaborating on our booklets, and now we were spending even more time together. We searched our hearts and God's, for just the right words and His perfect timing for these presentations, and always asked that His touch would be upon those who would hear us.

During those weeks and months, Steph was on a regimen of chemotherapy every three weeks, and the side effects took their toll, especially during the week of the treatments. Somehow, the Lord arranged it so that there was never a conflict with her chemo treatments, and we thanked Him every time for He never failed to bring her through.

Despite her illness, He continued to surprise us with new and thrilling adventures. Eventually, we were invited to be interviewed on the local Christian radio station by a friend of mine who had a weekly broadcast, and from that came new invitations to come and share at churches, Bible study groups and women's groups.

During one of our early dinners out, we had talked about a trip away from home. I had asked her what she would like to do. Her answer was so childlike.

"I just want to meet people", she said.

I had a wonderful idea! I knew of a place we could visit where she could meet believers *and* be filled with the beauty of God's creation at the same time! It was a beautiful place I had come to love and was somewhat familiar with, since there was nowhere else on earth I would rather visit. I wondered if I was being selfish by mentioning the city of my dreams: San Diego, California.

I told her about the flowers, the gorgeous blue skies, the majestic Pacific Ocean, the mountains and desert, the trolley, the plane trip! I have to be honest, I wanted to take her there more than anything.

It didn't take much to convince her and soon we had a date set in April. All we had to do was make the reservations and arrange for the care of our daughters. Oh, and one more thing — our vacation couldn't conflict with her chemotherapy treatments and so it had to be approved by her physician. Not a tall order for God, we knew, so we asked Him to arrange all the particulars if this trip was within His will.

I called Aubrey Beauchamp, Founder Coordinator of the USA Hospital Christian Fellowship or HCF, a couple weeks later to tell her about our plans for an April trip to her part of the world. She immediately invited us to speak at a Hospital Christian Fellowship retreat already planned for that exact same period of time. We accepted.

Once everything was in order, we made our plane reservations. It was a 'GO'! A couple days later, Aubrey called to tell us she had asked a friend who always arranged her travel schedule, to book us on a flight to California. It was all arranged! Then, to our excitement, we found out the flight she had booked us on was exactly the same one we had already decided on. In fact, it left us speechless!

God is a fantastic travel agent!

If there is one thing I would want to emphasize regarding Steph's ministry, it would be her *obedience to God*. Looking back now, I can see what a difficult time this could have been for Steph had she not chosen to listen and obey Him. In the natural, she was a young woman, newly widowed, raising a teenager alone and dealing with chemotherapy. That seems like enough of a burden for anyone, but Jesus has promised that His yoke is easy and His burden is light, and Steph took Him at His Word.

Burdens are only easy and light, of course, if we choose to let Him carry them for us, but we are forever taking them back. God understands us so well, and as He encourages us and waits for us to yield these burdens to Him again, we are developing and growing stronger in our faith. He is not condemning us for our humanness for He loves us too much for that. Besides, He knows our every weakness and strength and will not ask more of us than He knows we can carry.

If you believe He has asked you to do a specific task for Him, don't be afraid. Whether you think it is too big, too small, or even seems beyond your ability, please say "Yes!" and get ready for the ride of your life!

CHAPTER SEVEN

THE SHOP, THE SOUP,
THE SERVANTS

In three months time, our booklets were finished and at the proofreader's desk. Steph and I financed the printing ourselves, and planned to sell them at a minimum cost, enough to offset our original expenses, and after that, to deposit the money into a special HCF bank account.

When my friend Charlotte had died, a memorial fund had been established in her memory, appropriately called the Charlotte Shupe Memorial Fund. The intention was to financially assist others who wanted to attend various HCF seminars and conferences held across the USA. Though not a large sum of money, we had been able to provide funds for a number of people over the years, and wanted to continue this practice.

Our current HCF group, though small in numbers (five to be exact) was able to accomplish more than we had hoped for. We eventually provided assistance to many others who would attend various happenings in California, Pennsylvania and Kansas City including traveling expenses for Steph and I. We were even able to completely sponsor a trip to California for a young man from Kenya who was studying pharmacology in Philadelphia, Pennsylvania.

By the time the booklets were printed, it was springtime in Ohio, and the whirlwind of being a 'Heartwarmer' was just beginning. There was so much more to come! We saw that God was teaching us to be obedient to His direction, to simply follow the road signs along the way, and enjoy the ride!

Not too many people really knew what we were doing, but those who did, acknowledged God's hand on this budding ministry, covered us with prayer and became our encouragers as they cheered us on. Our support group consisted of our three daughters, Steph's parents, and our small, but vital HCF Bible Study group. As Zechariah reminds us:

> *"Not by might, nor by power, but by my Spirit, says the Lord of Hosts - you will succeed because of my Spirit, though you are few and weak".*
>
> (Zechariah 4:6)

Allow me to share with you what He can do with just a few weak and willing people. I think you will be astonished!

While I was still caring for my mother in January, Steph was taking her chemotherapy treatments and being led by God. Her little Heartwarmer cards were becoming more familiar locally as they were being seen in doctors' and hospital waiting rooms, dentist offices, the hospital chapel, and anywhere else God told her to place them.

Our friend, Dolores, a talented seamstress and reweaver, had offered to create a Heartwarmer wall hanging as a gift for Steph. Steph excitedly drew all the pattern pieces, and before we knew

it, these adorable items of applique on burlap were being produced. Dolores, who used two arm crutches to get around her
home, was able to sit at her sewing machine, and with nimble fingers create these beautiful hangings.

I had only one skill and that was decorating cakes. I wanted
to surprise Steph with a heart-shaped cake with the "Flowers For
My Friend" pattern as its decoration. Before long, I had orders for
more of these cakes, Dolores had orders for her wall hangings,
and Steph had orders for her cards. Mainly at this point in time,
we were ordering from each other, but what an encouragement
we were to each other, and especially to Steph.

It came as quite a surprise when I received one hundred bright
red aluminum heart-shaped cake pans with see-through lids — a
gift from Steph, along with a signed statement giving me rights to
use her Heartwarmers for my cakes, cookies, and candies. What
do you do with one hundred cake pans? You make cakes, of
course! Dolores was also given the rights to use Steph's
Heartwarmers for her sewing projects. To say that Steph was
encouraging is the bare minimum of expressions.

Steph began mentioning Dolores' long-held desire to have a
little gift shop in her home. Although she didn't get out too frequently, she was very well-known in the community for her
church work, sewing skills, and also as the very able president of
the Council for the Disabled. In her home she frequently wit-
nessed to her many visitors about her love for the Lord. Little
children were always dropping in to see Aunt Dolores and hear
about her best friend, Jesus. A gift shop could be a perfect addition to the garden she had planted...in her own home.

We began thinking and praying and planning. What would we
put in the gift shop? Where would it be located in Dolores' house?
Could Dolores manage it herself or would she need help? We
looked at each other and wondered too...what could I contribute?
Janet claimed she had no talent, but that was no reason not to be

a part of the shop, we said. She could invest in a few small items for resale. That sounded good, and before we knew it, Janet's items, Steph's cards, Dolores' wall hangings, and my cakes were all a part of the inventory.

The Heartwarmer Shoppe would be just a 'little stop along the way' where people could purchase small items to give away as they sought to touch lives for God. The other thought we had was to provide a place where they could stop in to "rest their weary souls." We decided to hold our HCF Bible Study meetings there every Wednesday and open it up to anyone.

Ideas were being generated almost faster than we could think, and the exciting part was that these ideas were being acted upon! It's one thing to have a dream, but the thrill is in the fulfillment of it, especially if it is from God. It seemed the more we talked, the more the ideas formed. We continued to pray about everything, as we did not want to go ahead of His plans for us.

We often pondered on how God could possibly use us and our meager abilities. God reminded me and I shared with my friends, a simple and easy-to-understand parable:

"Think of the ingredients for a cake. Flour, sugar, salt, baking powder, flavorings, eggs. A little here and a little there, and you have a cake. Alone or in the wrong combinations, there would be no cake. I have put you together in just the right combination to produce what delights Me".

We understood that language, and began to have a lot of fun. Most of the ideas came from Steph, who, we acknowledged, received them from God. On our own, we probably would not have experienced the excitement of being Heartwarmers, and we probably would have remained sincerely devoted to God, and our weekly Bible Study. But He had so much more in mind for this small group of women.

One of Steph's outreaches was her Living Bible ministry. She purchased them in quantity and gave them to people of all ages.

They were an important part of the shop's inventory. She had also taken time to tape record herself reading the scriptures, and these, too, were available to others on a library lending basis.

We also had many teaching, motivating, and music tapes that we loaned out. I remember the blessing my mother received as she lay in her hospital bed, listening to the soft, gentle voice of Steph reading the Bible to her. In Steph's own physical weakness, I imagine it took a lot for her to make these tapes, but how very special they were.

Eventually, a red phone which we called "the Heartline," was installed at the shop. It was another wonderful way to reach out and touch others. Not only was she a brilliant Bible student and teacher, but Dolores also had a quiet assuredness for those who sought her counsel. For addressing others' physical needs, donations of clothing, soup, and muffins were also a part of the Heartwarmer outreach.

Wanda was another special member of our Heartwarmer group. Besides going to nursing homes with Steph's clown, Wanda was linked with Steph in another separate and very special mission - a mission only given to a select few. It takes courage and a special person to enter into the life of a patient diagnosed with cancer. So often, the very word brings a sudden fear in the pit of one's stomach, and often renders us wordless at the most awkward times. Just when you want to say something, you find you can't say anything.

There are times when it is all right to be quiet.

Perhaps holding a person's hand is all that is needed. At other times he or she may really *want* to talk.

Wanda and Steph, as a unique team, were able to do this time and again. The secret is that often you don't have to say anything, and learning this provides a great relief to those who wish they could 'do something.'

Reaching out and touching lives is what Heartwarmers are all about. They allow you to step from your shadow of fear, and reach out with God's love into the shadow of another's fear. Steph and Wanda visited many cancer patients, often bringing little gifts or tokens of their concern.

Yet, most importantly, they brought God, who wants so much to be visible at times like these.

The Lord doesn't bless us all with the same gifts and abilities. If He did, perhaps we'd all be on the phone, counseling and praying for someone in crisis. But then, what would happen to the hungry or the needy neighbor? Although God generated so many of these thoughts in Steph's mind, He knew she could not possibly give her all to any one of them. She was, I believe, used by Him as the catalyst to show us the realm of possibilities, and that with His help, wonderful things can happen. She once said to me,

"Everything I am doing can be carried on by someone else".

If all this diversity sounds a little overwhelming, I can assure you, in the natural, it was. But in the spiritual realm, it was simply exciting and fun to see what God was able to do with five people who weren't any more than ordinary — and He added to our number those He chose.

Along with our daughters and Steph's parents, He brought us Amy with her beautiful singing voice, Nita, who lovingly handmade Heartwarmer dolls, and Marcie, who wrote beautiful Heartwarming stories. Later, Marcie's mother joined our little group, and lastly, there was our precious little one, Cathy, who was an R.N. We were so blessed!

We would frequently wonder, though not aloud, where all of this activity was leading. What would happen if God called Steph home?...the ultimate healing?

"Steph keeps us all going and is our inspiration, Lord, so what happens when she is gone from us?" I wondered.

Yes, she was our inspiration here on earth, but that was because she sought His purpose for her life and acted upon the direction God revealed to her. We needed to continually remind ourselves that she belonged to Him.

There will never be another Steph, true, but He is continually raising up His people to inspire others. His wonders are for us all, but we need to seek His will and wait for His guidance most expectantly. Steph often said,

"His miracles are out there. We just have to reach out and take hold of them".

These wonders aren't necessarily measured monetarily, nor by our strength. Rather, I believe, they are measured by our desire to go the distance with God (entering into a partnership with Him) willingly and sacrificially, if that is His choice for us. Ultimately the goal is to reach souls, demonstrate His love, and allow Him to be glorified in all things, according to His purpose. There are no 'small things' in Kingdom living, for He has His master plan written before we were born, and He will enable us to fulfill our purpose just as Paul tells us,

> *"It is God himself who has made us what we are and given us new lives from Christ Jesus; and long ago He planned that we should spend these lives in helping others".*

(Ephesians 2:10)

CHAPTER EIGHT

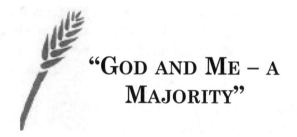

"GOD AND ME – A MAJORITY"

Steph's booklet for coping with long-term illness is called, *'O.K. God, Now What?'* and it has touched many lives. Her introduction says that she wanted to write a booklet of 'truths' that hopefully would help make the tense times somewhat more tolerable. She admits they are only suggestions – suggestions and an acknowledgement that you are not alone; that a smile can save the day and that an "I care" can do miracles.

Written as it is, by a cancer patient might lead one to think, 'Well, it's not for me. I'm in great health'. But I would submit to you that it *is* written for you, and yes, for me too. It is written for anyone with a heart for the sick and downhearted, and for anyone facing the most difficult and frightening days of his or her life. I can say this because I believe that by her written words, Steph allowed us to enter into her life in a far deeper way than we ordinarily are able.

Spending so much time with her during those two years gave me a lifetime of education, and most of it I received simply by watching and listening. This was her private world, tucked away from her children those many years ago, as she tried to protect them. Because she chose to share her thoughts with many of us, we have become privileged.

She found no magic cure for her illness or her broken heart... not here on earth, that is. But the One who was with her through these times taught her so much. I believe that more than anything else, she knew it was her mission in life to share this knowledge with each of us who still contemplate her words.

He taught her what one person, in sickness or in health, can do to make a difference in another's life.

God, the Creator of the universe, brought her into a unique partnership with Him.

How awesome!

When she felt sadness for her fellow patients and asked Him how she could reach out and touch them singularly for Him, He showed her. And together, they became a team.

"God and me...a majority!"

She learned also, not just by *giving* a smile, but also by *receiving* one, that lives could be touched *for* Him and *by* Him and that, either way, God was making a difference.

She received so much reassurance of her purpose in life by the words of John Henry Cardinal Newman and she repeated his statement every time we shared the Heartwarmer message:

I HAVE A MISSION

God has created me to do Him some definite service.
He has committed some work to me, which

He has not committed to another.
I have my mission.

I am a link in a chain, a bond of connection
between persons.
He has not created me for naught.
I shall do good. I shall do His work.

I shall be an angel of peace, a preacher of truth
In my own place while not intending it-
if I do but keep His commandments.
Therefore I will trust Him.

Whatever, wherever I am, I can never be thrown away.
If I am in sickness, my sickness may serve Him;
In perplexity, my perplexity may serve Him;
if I am in sorrow, my sorrow may serve Him.
He does nothing in vain, He knows what He is about.

She prayed the Serenity Prayer, which we all know, and love:
"God grant me the serenity to accept the things I cannot change, the courage to change the things I can, and the wisdom to know the difference".
She also asked the Lord to grant her the words of the prayer of St. Francis:

Lord!
Make me an instrument of thy peace,
Where there is hatred, let me sow love.
Where there is injury, pardon.
Where there is doubt, faith;
Where there is despair, hope;
Where there is darkness, light;
And where there is sadness, joy.

"O Divine Master, grant that I may not so much seek to be con-soled, as to console; to be understood, as to understand; to be loved, as to love, for it is in giving that we receive, it is in par-doning that we are pardoned, and it is in dying that we are born to eternal life".

God showed us through her life that no touch from Him is a small touch, and that a smile can make a difference. Her own unique gift, the Heartwarmers, have never been refused by any-one, to my knowledge, and I believe that is because God is the giver and we are the receivers. He enabled her to draw these lit-tle character cards, knowing she would never feel too 'grown-up' to tap a person on the shoulder and smilingly, without a word, give the little card away. He trusted her with a most childlike gift because He knows us so much better than we know ourselves.

"Suffer the little children to come unto me", Jesus said, "for of such is the Kingdom of Heaven".

(Matthew 19:14 KJV)

PART THREE

MONKEY SEEIN'
MONKEY DOIN'

CHAPTER NINE

A MOUNTAIN RETREAT

The day before we left for California was a busy and exciting one and non-stop from start to finish. For weeks, we had been buying clothes, packing, and making our plans for the 11-day trip away from home. Arrangements for the care of our daughters were one of our most important concerns, along with acceptable blood counts for Steph. She had a close call about two weeks before the trip when her white blood cell count dropped dangerously low from chemotherapy. But, thank God, after a brief hospitalization, it had risen to a level safe enough for her for travel. No chemotherapy for a few extra weeks was going to be a real treat for her. After her health status and our daughters' care were settled, we felt we could relax. I say that with tongue-in-cheek however, for it seemed we never relaxed in the physical sense of the word. In truth, we remained as busy as ever.

Since Steph was about to experience a time filled with more

than she had ever dreamed of, the most common question asked of her was,

"What are you going to do in San Diego?"

Almost everything we were going to do would be a first for Steph, from plane rides, buses, trolleys, and harbor cruises to mountains, beaches, and of course, the beautiful city of San Diego and the Pacific Ocean.

More importantly, I believe, was the fact that she was going to meet Aubrey, and also attend the retreat where she would meet many other people, just as she had wished for. However, when asked about her plans, she simply would reply,

"I'm going 'monkey seein', monkey doin' in California with Carol".

That remained her standard answer. So cute, I thought, and hence, the title for this most important section of the book.

On Monday, the day before we left, we hurried to the print shop to pick up the boxes of our booklets — hot off the press! What a thrill this was! We had already made a list of people we wanted to give copies to before we left - family members, doctors, nurses, and other close friends.

We were having a special HCF get-together at Steph's house that evening, and planned to give our faithful HCF family and our daughters their booklets then. In honor of Dolores' upcoming birthday, we had also planned a surprise cookout and birthday party for her. Dolores was thrilled and we all had a wonderful time.

Needless to say, Steph and I were barely able to sleep that night, and before we knew it 4:30 a.m. arrived and we were on our way to the airport.

The morning we were to fly to California, Steph had picked up her Bible, and it opened to Psalm 139. It spoke great things to her.

> *"Oh Lord, you have examined my heart and know*
> *everything about me. You know when I sit or stand.*
> *When far away You know my every thought. You chart*
> *the path ahead of me and tell me when to stop and rest.*
> *Every moment, You know where I am. You know what*
> *I am going to say before I even say it. You both pre-*
> *cede me and follow me and place Your hand of bless-*
> *ing upon my head.*
> *This is too glorious, too wonderful to believe!*
> *I can never be lost to Your Spirit!*
> *I can never get away from my God.*
> *If I go up to heaven You are there. If I go down to the*
> *place of the dead, You are there. If I ride the morning*
> *winds to the farthest oceans* (our trip to California),
> *even there Your hand will guide me, Your strength will*
> *support me. If I try to hide in the darkness, the night*
> *becomes light around me. For darkness cannot hide*
> *from God. Darkness and light are both alike to You".*
>
> (Psalm 139:1-12)

Psalm 139 became Steph's favorite Bible passage, and she counted heavily on every word. Thus, two years later, as she neared death, she told me to: "Tell people that God is there, Carol! He's in the trenches! Tell them this!"

Aubrey met us at the airport, and the memory of a chilly, rainy morning in Columbus, Ohio, quickly took a back seat to the beautiful blue sky and balmy weather of Southern California. We had lunch with some HCF friends at a Chinese restaurant in Seal Beach and then were off to Aubrey's home. Along the way, she treated us to her royal tour of Dana Point Harbor and the San Clemente Pier. Steph was thrilled at the sight of the magnificent blue Pacific Ocean, and equally wordless at the brilliance of all the colorful native flowers that seemed to be everywhere!

Bedtime was at 9 p.m. and after a 5:30 a.m. rising, we were soon bound for another thrill – a car ride up the I-5 freeway through Los Angeles along the San Gabriel Mountains. The mountains were so clear and green along the way! Aubrey explained to us that everything was exceptionally green this spring because the region had received more than the usual amount of rainfall that year. Steph was running out of words to express her feelings. She was speechless at every turn in the road. Up and over high hills (mountains, we Ohioans call them). As the sky filled with clouds against the blue, we saw hillsides with the orange, yellow and purple of millions of flowers not yet in full bloom. On the brilliant green hills, it appeared as though God had taken a paintbrush and marked them with pastel shades, causing us to wonder aloud,

"What must this look like when all the flowers are in full bloom?"

At dusk, we arrived at Hartland Conference Center set deep in the mountains. It was damp and chilly, having snowed a bit the day before, but soon we were gratefully snuggled in our beds and quickly fell fast asleep.

We slept peacefully all night, and awakened to the cracking, thunderous sound of huge trees falling to the forest floor. The lumberjacks had already been busy at work before we'd even opened our eyes! The sight and sounds of those giant trees being felled was unlike anything we'd ever seen or heard. How we wished for a way to capture it all, but, alas, we had no video camera or tape recorder available to us just then.

The meals were hearty, delicious, warm, and fattening! But, we thought (mischievously), very necessary to keep up our stamina in this cold mountain air. It was also a fine excuse to eat! We helped Aubrey with registration all day long, so we were quite busy, as there were seventy-seven attendees including ourselves. By bedtime, Steph was almost too tired to even take off her brand new wig, but she gave me fair warning before we went to sleep.

"If you see, hear, or feel anything flying across the room in the middle of the night, don't think it's a bat and try to kill it...it will be my wig!"

We laughed and agreed that a wig less than two weeks old could not be expected to become a beloved nighttime companion in such a short period of time.

The opening day of the retreat dawned beautifully and much warmer than the chilly, rainy day before. The topics for the day's program included 'Perspectives on Death', 'Sanctity of Life' and 'Dealing With Grief'. Since 'Caring to the End' was the retreat theme, these subjects were of course appropriate, and lovingly presented. Nevertheless, the care of the terminally ill caused much inner turmoil for the both of us. I can't speak for Steph, but I identified so much I felt I could cry for hours, as I thought of Charlotte, Dad, and then Mom. I soon began to concern myself with Steph's recent loss of Gary, as well as her own condition.

By 1:30 in the afternoon, Steph felt tired and went to lie down. I was totally wiped out by the emotions of the morning, and went outside to sit alone in the sun.

The next day, Saturday, was a little easier, due to the 'lighter' content of the messages that preceded ours.

Steph's testimony, given in her childlike way, wrenched the hearts of her listeners.

Steph lived the child-like faith for which we all must strive. We have been called to become like children; to have absolute joy in serving the Lord, to trust Him as our Daddy (Abba), and to believe and trust in His Word and promises.

I believe this was so evident as she shared her heart with the audience that day. Their response left us without words.

Our presentation had taken a slightly different direction from previous talks we had given, for this audience was practically 100 percent health care workers, and included social workers, doctors, nurses, hospice staff members, medical educators, dietary personnel, and home health nurses. I talked more about my association with HCF and also gave my personal testimony.

In her sweet and gentle way, Steph spoke eloquently and people were brought to tears (special 'Jesus' tears, we called them). We were so humbled by the responses of love, hugs and tears, along with the overwhelming feeling that God was doing a marvelous thing.

It was *His* day!

He had taken what Satan meant for evil and turned it into something beautiful! The love that was poured out cannot be described in words, and God received the glory!

Later, back in Ohio, we simply were never able to adequately explain to others when they asked about our retreat experience. It seemed impossible to relate this in our limited earthly language. Our prayers were that all who attended the retreat, ourselves included, would abide in the overwhelming power and peace felt that weekend.

We had made some cherished friendships, and left Hartland with hearts full of gratitude to God for allowing Steph such a wonderful opportunity to meet so many people—many more than she had ever hoped to meet.

I recalled when we were planning our trip I had asked her what she wanted to do if we did go on a vacation. Her answer had simply been,

"I want to meet people."

Well, she surely did, and many of them were blessed in return because of her request. It was such a simple desire, but I feel God is in the business of turning our most basic and simple requests into things of beauty and it is often His way of answering us.

We are told to ask expectantly. I'm not talking fancy cars and big bank accounts, though nothing is beyond His assets and abilities. Rather, I see Him receiving an equal amount of pleasure in granting even the simplest of requests. In the book of James we are given these words of wisdom,

"If you want to know what God wants you to do, ask Him, and He will gladly tell you, for He is always ready to give a bountiful supply of wisdom to tell all who ask Him; He will not resent it. But when you ask Him, be sure that you really expect Him to tell you, for a doubtful mind will be as unsettled as a wave of the sea that is driven and tossed by the wind, and every decision you then make will be uncertain, as you turn first this way, and then that. If you don't ask with faith, don't expect God to give you a solid answer".

(James 1:5-8)

He is, after all, the Giver of all good things.

"Be delighted in the Lord. Then He will give you your heart's desire".

(Psalm 37:4)

What is *your* heart's desire? Is it within His will? Is it according to His Word? Will granting your request bring Him glory, and honor His Son Jesus? If your answer is 'yes' then ask Him in love and trust and …

"May He grant you your heart's desires and fulfill all your plans".

(Psalm 20:4)

Chapter Ten

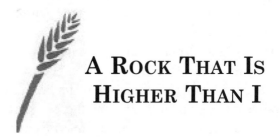

A Rock That Is Higher Than I

The retreat at Hartland ended at noon on Sunday, and as we left the area, Aubrey happily told us that she had another surprise in store for us. Her birthday was near and as a special treat, she had rented a cabin for us in nearby Sequoia National Park.

Higher and higher the car climbed up winding mountain roads. We arrived near suppertime and there on the grounds, near the office, were the largest trees in the world! They were huge beyond description - immense and gorgeous, with a reddish hue made even more intense by the sunshine.

With snow-topped mountains in the distance against a cloud-less blue sky, they appeared peaceful, yet so magnificent; they were simply mind-boggling. As I stared up, up, up at these majestic living things, Steph, ever the child, immediately ran to one of them and with arms outstretched as far as they could go, hugged one of those huge-beyond-words trees! I don't suppose I'll ever again witness such a sight, and I am so glad Aubrey captured the moment on film.

A later visit to the gargantuan General Sherman Sequoia Tree proved so exciting to us, as the famous Civil War general himself had grown up in our own city of Lancaster, Ohio.

The next morning as we awoke, we were again amazed at God bringing us here to this beautiful place. We ate our breakfast on the cabin's side porch and stared at the giant sequoia tree standing right beside us.

Steph, Aubrey, and I spent some time talking over breakfast. Steph shared some of her feelings regarding Gary's death, and I talked a bit about my father's illness and death. Mainly, our conversation was regarding nursing care, and those important special touches we had either observed during our loved one's dying days, or those we could only wish we had observed. A lot can be learned from the other side of the hospital bed, we concluded.

After packing the car, we bought some postcards and took a walk in a lovely meadow surrounded by trees of all sorts, including a grove of sequoias. We collected sequoia cones, which we later placed in small-capped jars, along with some sand and shells from the beach.

Trimmed later with a pretty ribbon, these became our home-made souvenirs – 'A Touch of California', for our friends back home. We also included a postcard with a painting of a shell, some sand and the ocean, and we added interesting facts about each item in the jar, such as the following about the sequoia:

> *The sequoia tree is the largest living thing on earth. The oldest trees are 3,000 years old or more. There are hundreds of thousands of cones per tree, and they are not much bigger than a leather button. Each cone contains 96 to 304 seeds, and there are approximately 3,000 seeds to an ounce.*

Our last stop before leaving the park was at the foot of gigantic Moro Rock. This monolithic rock outcropping lies 6,726 feet in the High Sierras, overlooking the Great Continental Divide, and the climb is ¼ mile up.

I found all of this most fascinating until someone suggested we climb to the top! Even the car trip up into the mountains had been almost more than I could bear. From such dizzying heights, the words "look down" are not even part of my vocabulary. I don't look down at miniscule forests, roadways, hills, and valleys! Instead, I look straight ahead or to the side of the road facing the good earth, but *never* toward the open side of the road, where there is nothing but space unless you look down, that is.

I learned another thing about myself on the ride up the mountains on our way to Hartland — I do not do well in the back seat, especially if I try to read or write in my journal. As much as I had wanted Steph to see all she could on the trip, I had to ask her to trade seats with me in order to ease my stomach's distress.

However, at the base of Moro Rock, Steph and Aubrey decided they would climb to the top, regardless of what I chose to do. My choices were to follow them and be scared to death or stay where I was. To remain behind meant I'd be denied the opportunity to see mountains with snow on their peaks, something I had wanted to see all my life.

"No way! This is definitely not for me," I thought.

The drive up the mountains had made me nauseous, so what would a climb up this rock do to me? I dreaded the thought. I looked at Steph fighting cancer, physically fragile, and yet so eager to start the climb. I felt embarrassed.

I am a seasoned "armchair" climber of some of the greatest mountains in the world... Mount Everest, Annapurna, and K2, among others. I love to read about alpine heroism and this type of adventure has always suited me well. To sit back in a recliner, wrapped in a blanket, sipping tea as I watch a great mountaineering effort on a rented DVD has always worked well for me. But, here, at the base of Moro Rock, I was being challenged in a new way.

As I looked again at Steph, something within me said, 'If Steph can do it, then so can you'. I saw that my fear was an emotional disability, not a physical one such as Steph endured. I decided to defeat my anxiety regarding heights and head for the top.

My courage was fleeting, but my determination a little more dogged. I had it all figured out — I would simply look nowhere but at the steps beneath my feet. 'Look at the ground', I reminded myself over and over. 'Don't look down the mountain, and don't look up, either. Just put one foot in front of the other, and try not to think about what you are doing. Hold onto the railings, one on each side. You can't fall if you hold on'.

I was acutely aware of Aubrey and Steph ahead of me. In fact, Steph actually reached the top first, though I didn't know that until I summited (mountaineering jargon).

Meanwhile the stone steps became a little narrower, which paradoxically seemed to give me an added sense of security, since I felt more enclosed by the railings I was gripping ever-so-tightly, all the while staring at the ground beneath my feet. The steps had been carved from this huge rock I was ascending and felt sturdy, solid, and powerful. I was the weak one, but here I was... still on my way up. I knew the top was nearer because the steps were becoming even more narrow. My stomach had been roiling about ever since I had started the climb, and it seemed to be in an even more delicate condition the higher I went.

Looking down to the ground as I had been, I happened to notice a small green lizard in the cleft of two rocks, secluded in their shadow. A Bible verse flashed into my mind; or was it a hymn? Something about being in the cleft of a rock... in the shelter of His wings… or was it about the shadow of a rock in a weary land? A rock higher than I? I can't remember now, but God had provided — as He always does.

These thoughts, along with the sight of the lizard, so tiny and vulnerable, yet shaded and protected from the sun, have never left me. God takes care of us, and overcomes all our fears, giving strength to the weary.

We all made it to the top, and Steph and I cried... that He is so enabling, overcoming all our physical and emotional limitations. I was able to see the Continental Divide and the mountains with the snow on their peaks glistening in the sun!

I was thrilled!

As I finally looked down from the heights of Moro Rock, everything below looking so small and almost level, the words of Isaiah seemed to echo in my ear.

> *"Let every valley be lifted up and every mountain and hill be made low. And let the rough ground become a plain and the rugged terrain become a broad valley. Then the glory of the Lord will be revealed!"*
>
> (Isaiah 40:40)

So it is with God and us. As we lean on His strength, the same thing happens spiritually. Because He goes before us through the mountains and valleys of our lives, the way seems so much easier to traverse; mountains are not so difficult to climb, and rough ground somehow is made smoother. How wonderful it seemed to me to be able to understand this.

Are you afraid of the mountains in your life?

As you hand these fears over to God, heed these words from Psalm 18 as you climb to new heights!

"This is too high, Lord. I'm afraid of getting hurt.*"*

> *"The Lord is my fort where I can enter and be safe;*
> *no one can follow me in and slay me. He is a rugged*
> *mountain where I can hide; He is my Savior. A rock*
> *where no one can reach me, and a tower of safety.*
> *He is my shield."*

                                        (Psalm 18:2)

"I feel weak in the knees, Lord, as I go higher and higher".

> *Now in Your strength I can scale any wall, attack any*
> *troupe.*

                                        (Psalm 18:29)

"I need to hide from these frightening heights!"

> *He is a shield for everyone who hides behind Him.*
> *For who is our God except our Lord? Who but He*
> *is a rock?*

                                        (Psalm 18:30-32)

"The higher I climb, the more rugged the peaks."

> *He gives me the surefootedness of a mountain goat*
> *up on the crags. He leads me safely along the tops*
> *of the cliffs.*

                                        (Psalm 18:33)

"The higher I climb, the narrower the path."

> *You have made wide steps beneath my feet so that I*
> *need never slip.*

                                        (Psalm 18:36)

CHAPTER ELEVEN

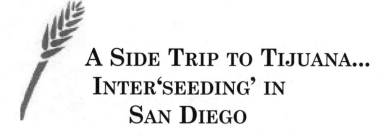

A SIDE TRIP TO TIJUANA... INTER'SEEDING' IN SAN DIEGO

We'd had a big day, full of the sights and sounds of San Diego, complete with a cloudless blue sky, a beautiful day full of fun, a city bus tour, shopping at Seaport Village, and finally an evening Harbor Dinner Cruise. As the cruise ship went beneath the lovely Coronado Bay Bridge, we discussed what we might do the next day, our last one in Southern California. I was worried about Steph's stamina, but she reminded me that she was checking everything out with God before deciding where to go, what to wear, what to eat, and where to stop and rest.

We were up early the next morning and headed across the street for a quick breakfast at a popular fast food establishment. It was practically empty, but one man definitely caught our attention. He was singing, and was very obviously a street person. We talked with him a bit, and for some unknown reason, he asked me if I was a nurse, which of course I confirmed. My journal tells me that we "talked of God". He also voiced his feelings regarding the mission where he stayed, telling us that he didn't like 'all those Mexicans' who stayed there at night. And with that said, he left the restaurant and returned to the streets.

By 8:30 a.m., we were on the trolley and headed south to the border town of San Ysidro. Had it been my choice, we'd have been sitting on a relaxing bus trip through the world famous San Diego Zoo...and we'd have never met Andy.

What follows are the happenings of that day, taken from my journal of April 24, 1986. It is an exciting adventure of God's very personal touch on our lives.

"Need some help, lady?"

Buying a one-dollar trolley ticket had never been a problem before, but for some reason, this morning, I needed help. I hadn't noticed, but the couple in front of me had lost their money in the ticket machine and now I had received one after inserting only fifty cents. I told Steph and she pointed out to me the couple who had lost their money trying to buy their ticket. I gave them their ticket and returned to try again.

The surprise offer for help had come from a young man, perhaps twenty years old, with short black hair, dressed in jeans and a tee shirt, carrying a book under his arm. I told him we wanted to take a trolley ride, but weren't sure where to go. I asked Steph,

"Where do you want to go? North to the zoo or south to Tijuana?"

I know she sent a quick prayer to God before happily replying, "Tijuana!"

I apologized to the young man for our brief indecision regarding our destination. He replied,

"That's all right, lady. This has already been a bad day for me. They cut my hair at the barber's today—it's never been this short".

He was obviously quite distressed by his haircut. Ever the

comedian, Steph piped up about her 'chemo hair-do', leaving our new friend confused, and me in stitches! There was only some peach fuzz beneath that attractively styled wig!

Finally, we boarded the bright red trolley on its way south to San Ysidro and the Mexican border. Our friend sat behind us and we talked. He suggested we might like a little visit to Imperial Beach later, and told us how to buy the bus ticket to go there from Iris Ave. He said he'd be going there later in the day. We also visited with the couple who had earlier lost the dollar in the ticket machine. They were from New York. (Steph reminded me later that trust was established earlier at the ticket machine when we returned their ticket to them). They were going to Tijuana also, and we agreed to share a cab to and from the Tijuana shopping area.

Later, we were able to get through customs with no waiting! (My notes reflect our gratitude: 'Steph very tired! God helped us through the border!')

We had an ice cream at McDonald's, but consequently missed our trolley. I learned there were trolleys every fifteen minutes, so I went to the ticket machine. This time, however, I had to buy a trolley ticket *and* a bus ticket.

Now, what had that young man told me to do?

I couldn't remember, and it was crowded with travelers and people buying tickets. In spite of the noise of the crowd, I heard a familiar voice say,

"I thought I told you how to do that, lady!"

Dumbstruck, I looked up and there was our friend again! Walking toward me, still with the book under his arm, he smiled and said he was going to Imperial Beach now, and that he'd help get us there, too.

"Just go with me", he said.

Gratefully, I accepted his help and hurried to get Steph.

Steph had suggested to me when we first arrived in San Diego, "You do the talkin' and I'll do the prayin'".

We had done so much in the days prior, and she felt she could best serve the Lord by 'prayin'.

That's O.K, I thought, as that will conserve her energy.

(I had much to learn about the power of the prayers of a silent prayer warrior.)

And so I talked.

His name was Andy. We talked all the way to Iris Ave., as well as on the bus ride to Imperial Beach. Steph silently prayed all the while. Andy was with the San Diego Job Corps, working to earn his GED, and was planning to join the military after that. With the Job Corps, he had found friends, a job, a place to live and, he hoped, a future.

"But", he told me, "someone set me up for something I didn't do, and now I have to leave the Job Corps".

Just the day before, he had been told he had to leave by Monday, and soon would have no job, no place to sleep, no money or food, and no friends to hang out with.

Earlier, he had told me he had been an orphan since age twelve and had lived off and on with an aunt and uncle in Arizona. He was just twenty years old, and now had a very uncertain future.

He mentioned that just the night before the Coronado Bay Bridge had looked very tempting to him. (Had he really been thinking of suicide?) I almost fell out of my seat to think how God had directed him to the trolley stop, not once, but twice that day. He had helped us, even though he was deeply distressed, and now I was able to tell him how God had been looking out for him, even in these worst of circumstances. When I told him Steph and I had been under the bridge the night before on a harbor cruise, he was amazed.

"Lady", he said," I've felt so much better since I met you both today".

Isn't God amazing in the ways He intertwines our lives? I silently thanked Him, and asked that He do the same for Steph's and my children — that He would always put the right people in their paths along life's way.

We transferred from the trolley to the bus, and were soon at Imperial Beach. Steph walked off a little way to look at the ocean and commune with God, and I had the opportunity to talk and pray with Andy.

Imagine!

He even asked me if I'd like to walk into the water with him! Off came the shoes and socks. I rolled up the cuffs of my slacks, and off we went!

It felt like a sacred moment to me, as we went into the ocean's water together — he, a twenty-year-old, and me, a forty-six-year-old grandmother. We prayed together as we walked back to the beach.

To this day, I am amazed at these events!

Back on shore, Andy remembered that he'd earned a lifesaving certificate during his time with the Job Corps, and said to me,

"Maybe I can get a job here at Imperial Beach until I can get things worked out".

Imperial Beach was, by the way, the beach where he had spent so many good times playing volleyball with his Job Corps friends. So that was why he wanted to go there today, I thought. Happy memories of days just past, but now, sadly, at an end. Andy also told me he was afraid to go back to Arizona because he used to be a gang leader there, and did not want to go back with the old crowd.

"I want to straighten out my life", he said.

He showed me the pictures in his wallet of his family, and mentioned that his Grandmother and sisters in Mexico 'have been praying for me all these years'.

"And God is honoring those prayers, even today, Andy", I said.

As we watched Steph at the ocean's shore, alone with her thoughts and with God, I told Andy a little about her. He was saddened as I told him about her husband Gary's death just six months earlier, and also that now she was facing a second battle with her own cancer. I told him about the Heartwarmers and about our booklets, and promised him that we would be praying for him every day. He expressed how grateful he would be for our prayers. Back at the bus stop as we hugged Andy goodbye, we gave him a Heartwarmer and a copy of Steph's booklet.

And speaking of books, remember the book he'd been carrying under his arm all day long? Well, it was not a schoolbook as I had supposed. Rather, it was a Gideon Bible, given to him the night before in San Diego. For instead of jumping from the Coronado Bay Bridge that night, he had gone, for some unknown reason, to a city mission. There he had been given not just food and a place to sleep, but, oh, so much more!

Don't you agree?

CHAPTER TWELVE

DR. DOBSON CALLING

Steph and I arrived back in Ohio tired, but so full of joy, and of course, happy to be reunited with our families. Our mailboxes already contained correspondence from our newly-made California friends. When I called Aubrey the next day, she had also received mail from some of the retreat attendees. She also asked if we would be able to return to California in the fall to speak at another retreat, and we excitedly accepted her invitation, contingent on Steph's health, of course.

Because of the extent to which HCF had grown since its inception in the USA in 1972, Aubrey now had a small staff, including a secretary named Carol, who came to her HCF office every day to help with the mounting amount of paperwork and phone calls. It had been fascinating to Steph and I to learn that Carol's son was employed as a sound technician by Dr. James Dobson's 'Focus on the Family' organization.

About a week after our return from California, Aubrey told me she had sent a copy of each of our booklets to Dr. Dobson's offices by way of Carol's son!

Now, *that* was just too exciting!

In fact, I don't even know how I responded to this information. I was probably speechless, or maybe I said something requiring no thought at all, such as, "Wow!" It was thrilling and certainly not something that either Steph nor I had even thought of. Besides, we knew we were not to promote ourselves in any way, but only to promote God in all things! Now, it seemed God was busy at work in a manner that came as a total surprise, for the connection between Aubrey's office and the staff of Dr. James Dobson hadn't even crossed our minds.

A little rest-time after our trip was in order, but it didn't last very long. Soon I was back to work, Steph was back on chemotherapy, and we both were trying to spend as much time with our families as possible. Laura and I had been living in a two-bedroom townhouse since my divorce, and I was finally beginning to feel I might be able to handle some increased responsibilities. I began looking into the possibility of buying a home of my own, but I wasn't sure if it was the right time yet for any major change in my life.

There were some cute little Victorian cottages for sale at the Lancaster Methodist Campground, a very historic little spot right inside the Lancaster city limits.

Steph, Amy, and I continued to receive invitations to speak, and also spent time writing to many of our new HCF friends in California. By the time our booklets were only two weeks old, we had deposited $270.00 in our HCF bank account. The Heartwarmer Shop was developing nicely, and new folks were attending our Bible Study on Wednesday afternoons.

One of the new people who came to our Bible Study was Steph's next-door neighbor, Jan, who owned and operated a monogram shop in a lovely and unique location in town. This was a small area, perhaps half a block square containing a cluster of boutique shops which were quite popular. People came from all around to spend the day in Lancaster to browse through the shops, have lunch, and enjoy the atmosphere. Jan's shop was located on the second floor of a large colonial house. The downstairs areas contained an interior decorating business, a stencil shop, and a doll and toyshop. It was a prime location.

On our last evening in San Diego, I had walked from our downtown hotel to the beautiful Horton Plaza, an open-air mall right in the center of downtown. It was alive with Mariachi bands and beautifully designed multi-leveled, multi-hued buildings. It was an Ohio visitor's dream! No mall in Ohio could ever be open to the air! It was festooned with colorful banners, hanging baskets of flowers of all shades and I fell in love with it. I happily climbed the stairs and rode the escalators up and down until I was certain I had seen all it had to offer.

Just before leaving the mall, the glint of silver and gold had caught my eye. There, in the center of the mall was a kiosk containing beautifully crafted jewelry, some hanging on chains and many others displayed on elegant black velveteen. The jewelry pieces were actual seashells and leaves, which had been electroplated in 24 carat gold or sterling silver. I was entranced, and it took awhile, but I finally decided on the piece I wanted to own. I settled on a highly polished white turbo shell edged in gold on an 18-inch chain. Back at the hotel, Steph was sleeping, but I eagerly rushed back to show her my find. A hurried return trip to the mall was my pleasure, as Steph wanted to purchase 3 more necklaces like mine for herself and her daughters.

Little did I know by the end of the year I would have my own business in the same boutique shop where Jan was located.

The jewelry was a big hit in Lancaster for no one had ever seen anything even remotely similar to these delicate pieces of nature. Steph suggested I could invest in a quantity and sell them. After some prayerful consideration I was, in short order, the happy owner of a large quantity of lovely shells and leaves, along with everything necessary to create earrings, necklaces, and stick pins.

Selling them literally out of my purse, and sometimes even off my neck, convinced me to obtain a vendor's license and seek an outlet for my little jewelry business. Jan, seeing an opportunity to help someone, offered to rent me some space in her shop, and before long, the jewelry, under the business name of '*My Father's World – Gifts of Nature*' was up and running.

Eventually, this little enterprise evolved into a three-room business located just across the hall from Jan, and included Christian gifts and books (food for the soul) and also a Garden Tea Room (food for the palate).

I had obtained a baker's license and my homemade cakes, candies, and cookies were soon displayed in glass showcases. I had used yellow and white lattice-styled wallpaper, along with round, white wicker tables and chairs. A bright grass-colored carpet and hanging green plants completed the outdoor theme, and Amy's beautifully framed photographs of nature's beauty adorned the walls.

Though the business operated for only a year, it was fun, and many times the Lord brought people there for spiritual rest and refreshment. He also used the Garden Tea Room to provide me with encouragement, as so many who came to shop or visit were specifically used by Him to meet my own needs. It was no coincidence that the first time I met Jan was through her special neighbor, Steph.

Both of our family responsibilities continued, along with all of our other activities. My teen-aged son Rob, who spent every other weekend with Laura and I, brought such joy to my life. But the joy also mingled with sadness at the cost parents and children pay for broken homes and marriages.

This being my second failed marriage, I often found myself dealing with feelings of inadequacy as a mother and a failure as a wife. My first two sons, adults by then, had to experience family breakups twice in their lives. At least I could console myself with the fact that they were adults by the time my second marriage ended, though nothing ever erased the guilt I felt.

For this reason, I was grateful to be so busy with work, the shop, the Heartwarmers, and mothering Laura and Rob as best I could, hoping that our time together was of the highest quality. We had the usual family problems to cope with as well as some great times.

Weekends with Rob meant hiking, fishing, and doing guy things whenever possible. On the opposite weekend, Laura would go to her Dad's farmhouse. That was when Steph and I had our special eating-out times.

Jim, my oldest son, was living in Lancaster, and only a phone call away. During my mother's illness, his past experience as an orderly in the hospital was very helpful, and I knew it was painful for him to see his Grandmother so ill. Laura of course was my first assistant and, at the tender age of twelve, did a wonderful job helping me.

Rob, coming every other weekend, spent time talking with Mom, too, and helping in any way he could. I am so grateful for his loving assistance.

My daughter-in-law Penny was especially close to us, and often stayed with Mom, enabling me to get away to the stores, etc.

I have wonderful memories of my first granddaughter, Jennifer, crawling about on Mom's bed. I can't imagine how much her precious presence ministered to my mother during this time.

The only son missing during those times was my second son, Scott, who was stationed far away in Japan while Mom was ill. When he finally was able to come home on leave, we had a wonderful family reunion. My children all stayed at my house and though there were enough bed spaces, in the middle of the night I found them all sprawled near each other in my living-room, fast asleep. My heart was filled with love as I looked at my children, so happy to be together at last that they wouldn't even go to bed. They just wanted to be together all night.

God seemed to remind me that this is His heart's desire also, that there was be a time for us all to come home to Him. We will be so overjoyed to be reunited with our loved ones again, just as God will be. He is not willing, however, that one of His children be missing from this great reunion, and He only asked me to do my best to help make this possible.

He is not willing that any be lost!

> *"Children are a gift from God - or like sharp arrows to defend him. Happy is the man who has his quiver full of them."*
>
> (Psalm 127)

I am sure this applies to mothers as well.

The trip Steph and I had taken blessed us beyond words, and yet, God had one more big surprise in store for us. I'd like to tell you how He did it. I believe our Father in Heaven takes great delight in pleasing His children, just as we parents do.

I always loved to have parties or to surprise my children and grandchildren, and would probably be far too extravagant if I had the means to be. The marvelous thing about God is that He knows when to say 'yes' and when to say 'no'. He also seems to enjoy delivering little surprise packages when we least expect them, and He can do it with something as simple as a phone call...

Our HCF group had decided that in addition to our Wednesday afternoon Bible Study at the Heartwarmer Shop, we would resume our evening study at Steph's house. That way, even if she weren't feeling well, she could be blessed by our fellowship and Dolores' teachings.

About three weeks after our return from California, we gathered at Steph's for a time of sharing and study. We handed out our handmade souvenirs of sand, shells and sequoia cones and eagerly answered all their questions about our experiences there.

I had received a note that very day from Aubrey telling Steph and I that Dr. Dobson's office had been trying to reach us! This was amazing to all of us. Aubrey also wrote that she had sent the audiotape of Steph's and my Heartwarmer presentation at Hartland to Dr. Dobson's staff.

Even as I was talking about this exciting and unexpected happening, Steph's phone rang! I jokingly said,

"Get the phone, Steph. It's probably Dr. Dobson".

Steph went to the kitchen to answer the phone and was back in the living-room with us in a split second, silently jumping up and down.

"What is going on with her?" we thought.

We soon found out, for she covered the mouthpiece with her hand, and excitedly squealed,

"It's them! It's Dr. Dobson's office and they want to talk to us! Here, Carol, talk to them!"

The phone was instantly placed in my hands. "Now what?" I thought. "How can I talk to these important Dr. Dobson people?" I was terrified and thrilled at the same time!

"Hello…this is Carol", I stated.

A friendly woman was on the other end of the line telling me 'they' had read our booklets and liked them very much.

"We think the Heartwarmer ministry is wonderful, and although we can't have you visit us personally at this time, we would like any audio tapes of you 'girls' speaking or being interviewed".

I told her that currently there were no other tapes available, but that we would send them if any were made in the future.

No sooner did I hang up then we breathlessly called Aubrey, saying,

"You won't believe this, but…"

For at least two minutes after these calls we looked at each other in total shock and eventually agreed,

"If that isn't evidence of God's perfect timing, then what is?"

As Steph's condition and energy waxed and waned throughout the year, this evening's encounter with the Dobson 'family' remained a highlight which lifted our hearts and brightened many of our days.

Eventually we were interviewed and audio taped at various seminars, but sadly we never followed up on the 'Focus on the Family' invitation. I can't explain why, but it was a missed opportunity, to be sure. Perhaps we thought it was too good to be true; or maybe that the quality of the tapes was not good enough. For reasons unknown, however, no further contact was ever made by us to 'Focus on the Family'.

It could be that an offer to do some work for God has come your way, just as it had to us through Dr. Dobson.

How much clearer could He have made it?

They called us from California the very minute we were talking about them! It was in God's design, but we did not choose to follow through and therefore never saw the other end of His exciting plan.

Whatever you do, don't close your eyes to God's plans for you, for they are never-ending and ever-rewarding. Don't do as we did and look at yourself alone, for this will put doubt in your mind.

When God comes knocking at your door, open it wide, and let Him come in with all that He has for you.

If you think you might bypass an opportunity due to fear or doubt, recruit all the prayer and support you can muster to help you take that first step and go for it!

We don't know what lies ahead, but, you know, it just might be a phone call...just for you!

Part Four

LIVING WITH DYING

CHAPTER THIRTEEN

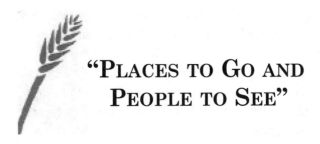

"PLACES TO GO AND PEOPLE TO SEE"

The rest of 1986 was filled to overflowing with blessings all around us. Besides the many requests to speak, Steph was often feeling well enough to go 'clowning'. As she joyfully and silently walked the halls of nursing homes, she would tenderly smile at the residents, give them a Heartwarmer or use her chalk to write the words 'Jesus loves you' on the small blackboard she carried. The numerous pockets of her clown outfit held many Heartwarmers - and so much love!

The National HCF Conference was to be held in July of that year in Kansas City, Missouri. Aubrey had asked Steph and me to bring Dolores as part of our Heartwarmer presentation. Dolores had been the grateful recipient of a beautiful, large sable-colored working dog named Clancy. He had been specifically trained to help only Dolores. We had often watched in amazement at Clancy's skill in helping Dolores to get dressed, bring the paper, and even pick up a dime from the carpet.

Aubrey asked that Dolores first give her personal testimony and then demonstrate Clancy's skills to the audience.   Steph and I were so happy that the Charlotte Shupe Memorial Fund had adequate funds to sponsor Dolores and Clancy for the conference, including her airfare. Dolores' eyes were overflowing with tears as the huge jet lifted off the ground in Columbus, Ohio, and climbed into the sky. She was seeing God's fantastic creation from four miles up in the air and it caused a precious release of her love and gratitude for her Maker. What a thrill it was for Steph and I to be observers.

While preparing for our trip to Kansas City, Steph told me that she felt the clown was supposed to go with us. We prayed about it and felt peace. We planned to do our usual presentation after Dolores and Clancy finished, and then in conclusion, I would explain about Steph's silent clown for God. It was a very special time.

When Steph finished, there wasn't a dry eye in the place.

After Steph passed away, Aubrey wrote a beautiful article in Steph's memory, and her moving description of the clown experience at the conference as taken from the memorial article follows:

> *That summer (1986) Steph and Carol were invited to share at the HCF National Jubilee Conference in Kansas City. Together with yet another Heartwarmer friend, Dolores, they spoke from their hearts and shared freely the love of the Lord. Stephanie distributed slips of paper, instructing the audience to write their 'burdens' down. She then slipped into her clown outfit and walked the aisles, smiling and touching everyone while picking up the slips of paper which she put in a basket.*
>
> *Using a feather duster, she then lightly swept over each*

outstretched palm, a gesture inspired by the Lord which visually affirmed the total removal of each one's burden.

She then returned to the stage, put the basket at the foot of a simple wooden cross and knelt before it in prayer.

It was a holy and unforgettable moment.

We came back to Columbus full of God's Holy Spirit and ready to go, wherever He chose. We did do a lot more traveling in-between her treatments, my working, and both of us juggling our time to also meet our family's needs. We made two short trips to Indiana to encourage smaller HCF groups and found this to be very rewarding.

Aubrey had also planned a series of seven fall seminars to be held in Indiana and Ohio over a two-week period. The topic was 'Spiritual Values in Health Care' and included emphasis on defining spiritual care, coping with grief, illness, death, and dying. 'Compassionate Care' was also a topic to be included in order to address the issue of that 'special touch' we all need and want to give.

Aubrey asked if we would be part of the seminar team, and asked Steph to include the clown. Our answer, as always, was dependent upon her health and making the proper arrangements for our daughters.

We were able to accomplish this mission, though it took a lot of traveling on our part. Rather than staying overnight out-of-town, we chose to return to our girls each evening whenever possible. We made it to all the seminars, staying out-of-town only twice. We put a lot of miles on the car — 2,200 in fact, but we did it! I am so glad, too, for it was soon time for Steph to began to slow down.

Even as the year was coming to an end, I detected a slowing of Steph's energy, more pallor to her skin, and evidence of joint pain as she moved about. She seemed tired all the time, and as we discussed her waning energy level, we also talked about our 'Energy Bank'. Knowing God will not give any of us more than we can bear, the plan was to be sure there was enough energy in the bank account before making a withdrawal.

We would ask God to search our hearts in order to determine if she was to make a withdrawal or not. We needed to know if He was requiring certain activities of her. It wouldn't be easy to decline invitations, but she had chemotherapy to deal with, and Tina to take care of.

God helped her prioritize by using the 'bank account picture', and it seemed to be a good idea. In talking about her tiredness, she shared with me how lonely it was because so few were able to acknowledge that she was weakening.

I felt weak inside as I listened to her and promised to be there for her, and with God's help I was able. There were times when she felt too sick to visit or go anywhere. I begged God not to take her home yet, for she still had 'places to go and people to see!'

When she felt well enough, we would talk and talk for hours and never run out of things to share. She talked a lot about the giving up of ourselves to God and about how much yielding He expects of us.

In the spring of 1987, she had been told she was in remission and could go off chemotherapy. That announcement had precipitated another series of deep discussions regarding a patient's right to be discouraged, even if he or she is in remission. Steph voiced some of her wonderings to me, such as,

"How do I know the doctor is telling me the truth? Why did he say I am depressed? Do I have a right to be depressed, even if I am in remission? As a Christian, do I have to live up to everyone else's expectations? I only feel good two hours a day — what more can I do? What more can I give up to God?"

I listened and tried to accept Steph 'right where she was' as Dr.

LeSar had always said. This didn't mean having all the answers, it simply meant being willing to walk alongside her and just be there for her. It was extremely painful to be as close to her as I was, seeing her so ill and yet struggling within herself. We prayed a lot, shared encouraging scriptures and listened to the beautiful music and singing of John Michael Talbot over and over again. One song in particular meant so much to us. It was from Jesus' own words as Talbot quoted the words of Isaiah.

> *The Spirit of the Lord is upon me; He has anointed me to preach Good News to the poor; He has sent me to heal the brokenhearted and to announce that captives shall be released and the blind shall see, that the downtrodden shall be freed from their oppressors, and that God is ready to give blessings to all who come to him.*
>
> (Isaiah 61:1-3)

These words fed our spirits over and over again, and gave us much peace.

Our daughters became like sisters also, and we often found them cuddled up together on the couch, fast asleep, the TV playing to no one. It was a tender, loving scene, and it is stored in my memory forever. God provided something special for these two young girls as Steph and I continued on the mission He had given us.

During Steph's better days, we still traveled and spoke, and she continued making visits to cancer patients with Wanda. Wanda recently told me of a situation that makes her cry even now, seventeen years later. She and Steph had gone to the home of a woman who was terminally ill. The room was dark, with shades pulled down, and the woman was lying in her bed, a turban covering her head.

They had a special time of sharing and encouragement.

The next time they visited this woman, about two weeks later, the turban was no longer covering her head and the shades were up, allowing the light and warmth of the sun to enter her bedroom. Steph had brought something for her—a stuffed toy clown as a gift of love. Weeks later, after she had passed away, the woman's daughter told Wanda that the woman's funeral service had to be delayed until someone was able to go home and return with the stuffed clown Steph had given her. It was tenderly placed in the casket with her.

It is easy to see the impact Steph and Wanda's visit had on this woman, and also to see the importance of a little stuffed clown when given in God's Name.

Back at the Heartwarmer Shop, our Bible Study group continued to meet, helping Dolores to manage the shop, loaning out books and tapes, and trying to reach out to others.

Steph's idea for a soup kitchen caught on and she and Wanda made pots and pots of soup, delivering it to shut-ins with Tina's help. Soon people were donating almost all of the necessary ingredients for the soup, and also the energy to assist in making and delivering it. During times like this, we would almost forget that Steph was sick. That was denial, of course, but it made the truth easier to bear somehow.

Earlier that same year, I was diagnosed with Epstein-Barr Syndrome or Chronic Fatigue Syndrome, as it is now termed. I was grateful that at least there was a name for all the aching muscles, lack of concentration, and indescribable exhaustion I had been experiencing. The Energy Bank was also applying to me. (In fact, it actually helped me identify in a very small way with Steph's profound tiredness.)

There was no treatment for my fatigue except vitamins and rest. I received this news just one week after the opening of my Garden Tea Room. Poor timing, I thought, for I had also just recently bought one of the little cottages in the historic Lancaster Campground.

Most of the cottages on the Campground are small, and though some are winterized, the majority are used in the late spring and throughout the summer. Many of the cottages actually evolved from the sites of early tents erected by those persons who came every year for the camp meetings so long ago. Sitting high on a hill, and overlooking a valley as it has for over one hundred years, it brings nostalgic memories to the many who grew up there or spent time as children and grandchildren of long ago residents.

A huge auditorium, a chapel in the woods, an historic reconstructed hotel, gift shop, museums and a pool make it a perfect location for those who enjoy strolling along the tree-shaded walkways of yesteryear.

The cottage I found was just right for Laura and me. My exhaustion, however, clouded my vision, causing me to see the opening of my Garden Tea Room and moving into a new home as mountains I could not climb. But God came to my rescue as family and friends who came to help me would prove!

Good days, bad days! Up and down days!

Steph and I kept on track by constantly communicating, mostly by telephone, sharing the latest neat things God was doing in our lives. We were often reminded of that which we already knew; there are scriptures to meet every single need we have, no matter how unique we may think they are. Steph and I practically 'lived' in the Psalms, but that was good, for it reminded us that King David also suffered from anxiety, fear, guilt, despair, sorrow, loss - the gamut of emotions. It is exciting to see that he triumphed over adversity time and again.

When he was broken, he wrote,

The Lord is close to the brokenhearted.

                                   (Psalm 34:18)

In his sadness and despair, he said,

> *I have wept until I am exhausted; my throat is dry and hoarse; my eyes are swollen with weeping, waiting for my God to act.*

(Psalm 69:3)

He also waited expectantly though he was downcast:

> *Take courage, my soul! Do you remember those times (but how could you ever forget them!) when you led a great procession to the Temple on festival days, singing with joy, praising the Lord? Why then be downcast? Why be discouraged and sad? Hope in God! I shall yet praise Him again. Yes, I shall again praise Him for His help.*

(Psalm 42:4, 5)

He experienced deliverance from his despair:

> *I waited patiently for God to help me; then he listened and heard my cry.*

(Psalm 40:1)

That same chapter tells us,

> *He has given me a new song to sing, of praises to our God. Now many will hear of the glorious things He did for me, and stand in awe before the Lord, and put their trust in Him.*

(Psalm 40:1)

Finally, David promised to tell everyone about the goodness of God,

> *Oh, Lord, I will praise you with all of my heart, and tell everyone about the marvelous things you do.*

(Psalm 9:1)

By the fall of 1987, it was evident Steph couldn't physically continue as she had been. She was back on chemotherapy, and enduring increased pain. More and more time was spent at home, conserving her strength for her precious family. I had to limit my visits with her also, for I knew it was time for Steph and her loved ones to be together.

This was very difficult for me to do.

We still had so much more that we wanted to do and talk about, and it seemed our partnership had just begun. Steph knew that she could call me any time of the day or night and that I would help her in any way possible. Whether it was a medical, emotional or spiritual need, I told her I'd be there for her. She had a wonderfully supportive family and loads of friends, and I was just one of many who loved her.

One instance stands out in my mind as uniquely special and planned by God.

She had gone to the Emergency Room with a sense of impending doom, a very frightening and real experience for many people. It just so happened that Dr. LeSar was on call that afternoon. Though he had met her just briefly one other time, I knew a spiritual connection would occur that day in the Emergency Room.

He spent three hours of his Sunday sitting in a chair behind the curtain in the Emergency Room with my friend, for after he had assessed her physical needs, he had remained to talk, and to comfort her. The only thing she ever told me about that special time with Dr. LeSar was that they had talked about things of a spiritual nature.

"How very like him," I thought, as I remembered the many times he had sat by my mother's hospital bed, held her hand and looked into her eyes before ever saying a word. God has given this physician the words to say to his sick and dying patients, and I believe he has been gifted by God to be a mediator for Him at such special times. Many are the days I have seen him walk the halls of our hospital, shoulders weighted down, I am sure, by the burdens of sadness he must bear. He once told me,

"It is a high price that is paid for those of us who choose to enter into another's pain".

I urge you to take the same risk — hold someone's hand, look into their eyes, and simply say, "God is here this very minute", for you will be bringing Him along as you enter the door of another's heart.

CHAPTER FOURTEEN

SAYING GOODBYE

My Mom and I never really said 'Goodbye' though our final separation was a long time coming. There were brief periods when we almost talked about where her illness was taking her. For the most part, though, my mother kept her thoughts to herself and therefore I was excluded. Throughout the final months of her life as she lay in the hospital bed in my dining room, I would wonder what she was thinking about.

I have made a life-long habit of trying to identify with the other person, be it a relative, friend, or patient; to enter into his or her situation as wholly as I possibly could. Why I started doing this, I don't know, but I know I felt I could empathize with that person so much more by using this self-created tool than I could without it. Yet, it often failed me, for I tended to get carried away as I tried to envision the situation from another's point of view.

More frequently than not, I allowed my mind to expand everything out of proportion. I have paid a dear price for assuming

I could enter into another's private world, realizing that by not wanting to demean the person or the situation, I may have done just that. I found I was not acknowledging the individual and the sum of all of his or her experiences, personal strengths, and goals. I now recognize it is impossible to do this.

In fact, in caring for my mother, this approach did not help at all. Could it be that my mother, by keeping me out, had come up with the means by which she could protect me? The thought never occurred to me at the time, for I was trying earnestly to be both daughter and nurse to her,though it has since been offered as a suggestion by friends and relatives who wanted to help me deal with this exclusion by her.

My parents had never shared their deeper thoughts with my brother and I when we were children, or even later as we became adults. It was the old way, I believe, of maintaining a separation between adults and children. Certain areas were simply 'off limits' and that included their bedroom, finances, political persuasions, and especially their decisions on any matter concerning our lives. You only entered these areas on invitation. As a result of this attitude, the 'doorway' to my Mom was basically closed before I even tried to enter it. Sadly, living with and caring for my mother allowed so much time for sharing about the past, reliving her childhood or mine, and possibly even voicing her fears.

It never happened, however.

As early as two months prior to her death, Dr. LeSar had urged me to write down what she said. In my journal of November 22, 1985, I wrote this comment,

She says nothing.

This tells me more in retrospect about accepting people right where they are, as Dr. LeSar had often advised me. I needed a constant reminder to do that, for it was difficult to do on a day-to-day basis. My hands were tied as I attempted to breach this wall of silence. I would wonder what I did wrong to deserve 'the wall', and though I'd try different approaches, it was to no avail.

I found was able to accept her anger at her diagnosis, at her treatments, at her doctor, and even at her nurse (myself), but I could not accept any anger toward her daughter (also myself). I could understand why dark depression could assail her mind as she lay there for days and nights on end. I could even understand her lack of appetite due to medications, inactivity or depression. On a few occasions, her steroid-induced cravings for lasagna, of all things, yielded some much-needed laughter. One day in particular, she asked if I could go to the store and buy some frozen lasagna.

"Sure I will", I said, "as soon as I can get someone to stay with you while I shop". Satisfied with my answer, she closed her eyes and went off to sleep, dreaming I am sure of steaming hot layers of lasagna noodles embedded with wonderful combinations of meat sauce and cheeses.

Shortly after dozing off, she awakened with apparently just one thought on her mind. She immediately asked me,

"Did you make the lasagna yet, honey?"

I am thinking that the aroma was just that real and overwhelmingly tempting as she awoke from her nap! Such moments brought a sweet respite from the downside in which we all existed.

By late January, her level of pain had increased, and she finally agreed to allow the Visiting Nurses to come to the house to help me with the care and management of her pain. I had waited for her to make this decision, as this allowed her some control over her life.

As she became weaker, it cut to the depths of my heart to watch as she tried so hard to use what little independence she had left, by adjusting the bed controls, holding a glass of water, picking up her pills, and feeding herself, all with trembling hands and severely weakened muscles.

How I hurt inside!

I cried as she gave me a hug one day, patting my back as if I were a baby and telling me,

"It's all right to cry for Mommy, honey, it's all right".

A sobbing child, being comforted by her dying mother. The child is thinking to herself. *'Soon I will never feel this embrace again'.*

Indeed, it was to be the last embrace.

Disorientation developed due to her elevated body temperature which vacillated between one hundred and one hundred three degrees, even higher at times. Care of her bodily needs increased each day, and God brought extra help by way of my brother Alec and his wife Lois, my daughter-in-law Penny, and my nursing friends. My stress and physical exhaustion melded into one, affecting my reasoning powers, decision-making abilities, and my emotional stamina. My mother's confusion only served to produce confusion in me.

"Why did she knock the things off her bedside table? Why did she try to put in her dentures upside down? Why is she incontinent? What can I do?" I cried.

God answered: "Allow Me."

Three days before she died, my mother had complained of left shoulder pain that radiated across her chest. She told me she just wanted to die, but the nurse in me needed to assess this pain. Was it her heart? Was it from sleeping too long on her side? Was the cancer now in her bones?

I asked some nurse-type questions which immediately resulted in anger toward me. She told me to stop looking at her, and that I asked too many questions. I had a hard time with these comments and her angry tone and besides, she was interrupting my very important assessment of her pain! I told her defensively I didn't know how I could take care of her if I couldn't ask any questions.

I cried in sorrow for my response to my precious mother, and also for hers to me. My hands were tied, and now, I had the added burden of guilt for my outburst.

"She's angry due to the pain," the VNA nurse said. Thankfully, she had brought liquid morphine along with her that day.

She sat beside me, promising that Mom's pain would soon be relieved. My mother, however, refused all other medications and said to me, (with what I perceived as hatred in her eyes).

"I'm sick of hearing your voice".

She then closed her eyes and shut me out at the same time. I still did not know what I had done wrong, and in my bewildered state of mind, felt that everything she said or did toward me was deliberate. I knew she was dying, and yet the defense mechanism and anger grew within me.

Along with the care of my mother, I also had the responsibility of keeping everyone in the family aware of her condition. This included calling her sisters in Maryland who were in complete denial, family members in other states, and also my son, Scott, who was stationed in Japan with the Navy, saying over and over the latest report (nurse taking over). My brother and I needed to be making funeral plans, the visiting nurse had suggested. It hadn't even crossed my mind.

My goal now was to be sure my mother received the best of care; that everything possible was done, but by someone else. I avoided my usual offerings of medications, sips of water, turning her, or any other comfort measures. Her physical care was taken out of my hands, and I was so grateful, for I didn't want my mother to die in anger. I didn't want to talk to anyone, but the next morning Laura called Steph, who immediately contacted our Bible Study group for prayer. What a fool I was, I thought later, not to have called my friends to ask for help.

Early the next day, Janet called and told me she was bringing lunch and planned to stay all day. She was such a wonderful help. Just being able to talk to her and share my burden of heartache was such a comfort to me! Her support was invaluable. Lois, my sister-in-law, called saying she would be coming that evening with her suitcase and planned to stay for as long as I needed her. Someone to take my place!

"Thank you, Lord!"

When Lois arrived that night, Mom said, "Hi, honey," to her, but hadn't acknowledged me all day! I was so angry! I remember what I said as I walked past her bed into the kitchen.

"I'm sure glad someone is 'honey' around here!"

Later, I wondered how I could have acted like that, but all I knew at the time was that I was hurting.

I had shared my distress over this incident with Stephanie earlier. Her advice to me was that I must sit down and talk to Mom about how she had hurt my feelings by rejecting me, and that I knew she loved me. I needed to tell her I was sorry for having snapped at her, to tell her how much I loved her, and to say what a privilege it was to take care of her!

I followed her advice and will be forever grateful for the gentle prodding of my special friend. In my state of mind, I may not have done anything for fear of provoking anger in my mother. It was clear to this nurse's mind that Mom was dying – that part of me was still working, under par for the most part, but still working. The daughter part of me had become immobilized.

I was incapable of initiating this time of saying goodbye, but I was able to follow Steph's direction. I didn't know what to say, so I used the words Steph gave me. I believe it took much courage for Steph to firmly tell me what I needed to do, but she was right, of course. I didn't realize that this was to be our goodbye time.

My mother died peacefully the next morning, my brother sitting by her bed holding her frail hand, tears coursing down his face. It was a fitting farewell to a wonderful mother.

I'll see you soon, Mom...I love you.

Dear Lord, I pray that You will be our guide, controlling our thoughts, words, and actions, should we find ourselves in similar circumstances. Make a way, using each of us as Your humble servants, to reach out in compassion to the hurting and the grieving. Help us not to fear what we will say, for it is You who wishes to speak at such times. There are no human ways to enter into these areas without the touch of Your Holy Spirit, and I believe You will give us utterance, and grant the healing. Amen.

CHAPTER FIFTEEN

THE GOD OF ALL COMFORT

Comfort, comfort, ye my people.... These words some-how whispered in my ears, over and over during that last week of my mother's life. I knew that soon I would no longer have a chance to talk with her at all, as she was slowly slipping into a semi-conscious state. Even though as a nurse I knew what was happening to her mind and body, somehow I was unable to reconcile this reality. One minute the daughter in me said, "Why won't she talk to me? Why is she acting confused? Is she mad at me? Did I say or do something wrong?"

The next minute I was assessing my patient, watching carefully her urinary output and listening for bowel sounds. I didn't realize the toll the twenty-four-hours-a-day care was taking on my own mind and body. When she refused her oral medications, I remembered her recent outcry to me,

"You ask too many questions!"

She really never talked to me after that and in a desperate

move to avoid angering her in her illness, I asked Laura to get up in the middle of the night to give her Granny her medicine. Laura did just that and it was shortly after that my sister-in-law Lois told me she was bringing her suitcase and would be staying for 'as long as necessary'.

How grateful I was!

I was counting on God's promises day and night, and believed very strongly that He would see us through these troubled waters.

> *When you go through deep waters and great trouble, I will be with you.*
>
> (Isaiah 43:2)

He is the Great Comforter and I knew He would provide the support and comfort we needed. So, when the words, *Comfort, comfort, ye my people* came to my mind, I knew He was speaking to my spirit with words of assurance. I knew it was scripture, but had no idea where to find it in the Bible.

During warmer weather, when she was a little stronger, Mom had spent weekends with Lois and my brother at their farm nearby. But as winter approached and the days grew colder and shorter, her strength, too, seemed to be diminishing, and she became confined to my home and her bed.

Counting on the Lord, I often wondered just how He would touch our lives during this time. It is extremely painful to watch someone you love die day-by-day, and this pain was a constant reminder of my father's death from cancer just a few years before.

But our Lord, the God of all comfort, brought peace to each situation as only He can do, and I would like to share with you how He touched me in a most profound way both before and even after she died.

The words of scripture were not intrusive, yet were always

there that last week, gently in my mind, calming me, and causing me to wonder what His message was to me. I even asked some friends if they knew where in the Bible I could find this verse, but no one had the answer. In retrospect, I believe He wanted me to receive the blessing of these words without any effort on my part.

I was exhausted and wrought with sadness and He knew what I needed. When Dr. LeSar came to spend time with her the night before she died, I shared this scripture experience with him as he was leaving. His eyes watered a bit as he said,

"I don't know why all this is happening, but I do believe you have a mission, and God will use all of this sadness and pain for good some day".

I believe now, so many years later, that I do have a mission, and that we all have a mission and only have to be willing to do what He asks of us in order to fulfill it. I believe mine is to write this book, and in doing so, show others God's wondrous love and compassion, which He exhibits in our lives when it would appear He is not there.

We took my mother's body back to Pennsylvania, and a week later, feeling so alone in my living room, I thought to use a concordance to search for the words God had given me. They are the first words of a beautiful chapter of the Bible–

> *Comfort, oh comfort my people, says your God. Speak tenderly to Jerusalem and tell her that her sad days are gone.*
>
> (Isaiah 40:1)

I was astounded as I read the entire chapter, crying and yet drinking in the beautiful words of assurance, and especially as I read the closing wonderful promise.

> *But they that wait upon the Lord shall renew their strength. They shall mount up with wings like eagles;*

they shall run and not be weary; they shall walk and
not faint.

(Isaiah 40:31)

My mother had lost the use of most of her muscles from a secondary illness related to the cancer, and so these last verses were especially meaningful. What a magnificent promise!!

However, this wonderful story does not end here. As I have previously written, God provided His comfort even after my mother's death. For far away, across the Atlantic Ocean in Italy, He had spoken these very same words to my friend Wanda.

I met Wanda when I first was introduced to Hospital Christian Fellowship in 1981. She was a full time staff worker for the USA HCF and was very sensitive to the prompting of the Holy Spirit. I had seen this evidenced on many occasions, and again on January 30, as she heard Him and obeyed.

Here is an excerpt from my journal dated February 10, 1986: '...cleaning up the house, rearranging the furniture, and returning hospital equipment, I became so sad and down, especially after going through Mom's desk. I received a letter from Wanda S. in Italy today that was written the day Mom died!' She wrote:

My dear sister,

The Lord put you in my heart this evening and I'm so glad, because I felt I must write, and tell you of His love for you – this day, this minute, our loving Father knows every heartache you've gone through - in relationships, in losing loved ones, and in even the frustrations of this day.

Through these times, He has been your strength, even before you knew Him, and now as Isaiah 40:31 says:

...but those who hope in the Lord will renew their
strength, they will soar on wings like eagles; they will

run and not grow weary, they will walk and not faint.

So soar my sister! The strength you continue in is not your own.

I was overwhelmed! I cried and thanked the Lord for His very specific and personal comfort for me. I was awestruck at how God was able to reach across the earth the very day my mother died and use an obedient servant to continue to reveal His comfort to me. Had Wanda chosen not to write me, this could not have happened and it reminds us all to listen carefully and obey His promptings.

> *What a wonderful God we have—He is the Father of our Lord Jesus Christ, the source of all mercy, and the One who so wonderfully comforts and strengthens us in our hardships and trials. And why does He do this? So that when others are troubled, needing our sympathy and encouragement, we can pass on to them this same help and comfort God has given us.*
>
> (II Corinthians 1:3-4)

We are able to share with others what God has done for us and encourage them. I have shared this experience with many over the years, and yet, I am overwhelmed with His greatness again and again! I have Wanda's letter in front of me as I type this and it is astounding! Not to be kept in a box, but to be shared with as many as will listen!

I am so glad I have been able to share this with you, the reader. God bless you.

CHAPTER SIXTEEN

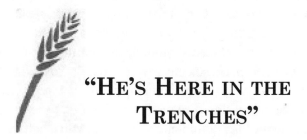

"HE'S HERE IN THE TRENCHES"

By September 1987, Steph's condition had worsened, necessitating morphine every three hours, and also a hospital bed at home for comfort. Steph, Amy, and I had been asked to speak on December 3rd at the church Amy and I attended and our prayers for Steph were intense.

"Oh, Lord", I prayed, "can we take Steph to speak at the church with us, too? Will she still be with us or be with You? Please prepare us all if You are going to take her home. Bless and keep her children and parents in Your loving arms. We all love her so. Please give us the strength to 'be there' for her during this time."

The next day after praying this prayer, I took salads for us to her home. We had a great visit, much like the old times, sharing so much and never running out of things to talk about, especially spiritual things. We prayed for more times like this. I worried about tiring her out, or taking time from my daughter, who needed me, or her daughters, who needed her more and more each day.

I was missing those hours and hours in which the Lord had revealed so much to us, affirming our friendship and its purpose over and over again. I found myself questioning Him about what would happen when she was gone. Losing my friend was too painful to consider. He had blessed us with countless hours together and, we both believed, had compacted this time to equal a lifetime of friendship — for His purpose.

By the middle of October, our time together lessened, as I felt the importance of giving up my time with her to her family. I was missing Charlotte, my Dad, my Mother, and fearing the impending loss of Stephanie. Her chest x-rays were looking worse, her blood counts were down due to chemotherapy, and her need for pain medication was increasing. I prayed constantly that she not suffer and often thought of her comment to me a year and a half earlier at the Hartland Retreat in California. The theme had been 'Caring to the End', and when Joyce, a hospice nurse discussed effective pain control, Stephanie had nudged me and said,

"Remember that".

It had hit me like a ton of bricks, for I did not often think of the possibility of her dying.

Early November found her doing well on 80 mg. of morphine every three hours. Just what did that mean?

To me — the nurse — it was a very large dose of morphine, and it meant she was in severe pain.

To me — the friend — and to others, it meant she was able to be up, take a shower, and then rest, perhaps allowing her to have a visitor for a short period of time. Her medication was adjusted frequently and eventually this problem would necessitate a hospital admission.

On December 3rd, after a brief stay in our local hospital, Steph was admitted to a Columbus hospital for further evaluation of her pain. That was the same day she, Amy, and I had been scheduled to speak to four different women's groups at the church in Lancaster, Ohio.

Amy and I would be going without Steph, brokenhearted, and yet not alone but with God. We knew He would still do wonderful things. Throughout the day, at home alone, I prayed,

"Fill us up, Lord, be our strength and let us be your instruments. We will go where You want us to go".

Even as I prayed that day, the only thought I had was:

"Tell them I am here".

Just as I was leaving the house, Steph called with a praise report! Her doctor was going to medicate her until the pain was gone! She was giving out Heartwarmers! And she said:

"Tell them all tonight that God is here — among the trenches."

When Amy and I sat in the car to pray before going into the church, she, told me she had already planned what she was going to sing, but had been thinking about another song, 'Thou Art There', all day. She thought she was supposed to sing it instead, but had been unable to find the music. She told me the words were perfect, about His being there with us, and 'where can we go to escape Him? Nowhere!'

I knew what she was saying! It was Steph's favorite, Psalm 139, in which David says just that — no matter where we go, He is always there!

Amy told me later how awesome it was to see the look on my face as she was telling me about the song. She had no idea it was Steph's favorite. We were amazed as we agreed that God had provided us with the evening's message: He is here with us always, no matter what the circumstances.

So we prayed she could find the music in the church, and if it wasn't there and God wanted her to sing it, to help her know the words and she would sing it acapella.

And that's just what she did.

She sang straight from the King James Bible! It was beautiful and I could see Steph at that hospital just 30 miles away with no darkness around her — only His light!

Not only did God make sure we understood the message we were to share that evening, but He also allowed us to experience this truth as we received those assuring words regarding our beloved friend. He had perfectly orchestrated our thoughts so that we did not misunderstand His plan. He did this through Steph's earlier praise report that 'He's here in the trenches,' through Amy's awareness of the song she was to sing, and through the thought He had put on my mind all day to 'tell them I'm here'.

Many years later, Amy was to say about this event,

"Isn't God amazing? No matter how many times this kind of thing happens, it is still so humbling that God chooses to reveal Himself in so many ways to us."

He wants to use us to show others that He is here with us, no matter the darkness, never leaving or forsaking us. He has given us His promises to hold onto for,

> *All His promises are true!*

(Psalm 18:30)

> *All His promises are backed by the honor of His name.*
> (Psalm 138:2)

His realm is not just in the natural, but in the supernatural also. He will guide and direct us to do His work here on this earth as long as we believe in His Word and are willing to hear and obey Him.

Listen closely, read His Word, share your sorrows and your praise reports with others too, for the…

> *Lord inhabits the praises of His people.*

(Psalm 22:4)

God enters into every second of our lives!
How exciting to be His!

CHAPTER SEVENTEEN

"FOLLOW ME!"

My home health assignments for the day included a home visit to Mr. Boone at his daughter's home on Paradise Road, a lovely country lane in Fairfield County. The twelve-mile trip from the office in the city was one of my favorites as it meandered in and around hills and valleys, and allowed me an opportunity to once again reflect on the beauty of the landscape. Watching for local wildlife was fun too, and, of course it gave me time to consider my patient and his needs. I always tried to remember each day before work to ask the Lord to open the door to any opportunity for me to witness for Him to whomever crossed my path.

Today, however, the Lord would cross my path instead, and in the most unexpected way. It would be several years, however, before I would actually see the end result of His plan.

Mr. Boone's daughter, Joyce, met me at the door of her lovely rustic home. We introduced ourselves and as I entered the house, I was taken by the many artistic and creative touches that had been used in its décor. I immediately felt at home. She escorted me through the house to her father's bedroom. Along the way, I noticed a beautiful painting of Jesus on the wall, and also some smaller sizes of the same painting which, I assumed, were prints. Jesus' smiling eyes beckoned me, and I made a mental note to ask Joyce about the painting after I had visited her father.

Mr. Boone was a kind, elderly gentleman. I enjoyed talking with both him and his daughter about his medical concerns, medications, and general state of health. A brief chat finalized the visit, and I promised to return within a few days.

Walking back through the house, again aware of the smiling eyes of Jesus in the portrait, I asked Joyce about its origin. She told me she had been commissioned by a gentleman from Columbus to paint Jesus in such a way as to show a 'relatable' Christ, one which today's young people could connect with. He was painted with a smile that continued up to His eyes; eyes that looked straight at the viewer with an expression of listening and gratitude. The portrait had been named, 'Follow Me' in reference to Matthew 4:19.

> *Then He said to them, "Follow Me, and I will make you fishers of men.*
> (Matthew 4:19 New King James Version)

I commented on how beautiful it was, and Joyce offered me a number of wallet-sized copies, along with some church bulletins, which also had the painting on the cover. I remember how excited I was to receive these. Joyce also told me that she had been able to share Christ with others by giving her artistic chalk-talks.

I felt our HCF Bible Study would be a perfect venue for her presentation, and asked her to speak to us soon. She accepted my offer and we agreed on a mutual date to be confirmed within the week. That night, I framed one of the 5"x7"prints for my home, and put a few wallet size ones in my purse to give away.

What a special blessing, I thought. This picture makes me feel so loved and warm inside. Just look at His eyes! He loves me a lot! It felt so good.

I hung the framed picture on my wall and it has been there ever since.

Later, I gave Steph a framed picture as well. She had often admired mine, and since we frequently gave each other little tokens of our friendship, it seemed a perfect gift. She told me later how much comfort it gave her, and I agreed it did the same for me.

Steph took the picture of Jesus with her when she was admitted to the hospital for the last time. It was in an acrylic frame that stood up on her bedside table, in the same way that her little Heartwarmer cards stood up. The hospital admission was for pain management, as the methods used at home were no longer effective. Groggy, she told me, she was so concerned about remembering everything God was doing.

Despite the doctor's best efforts, though, substantial pain relief remained elusive.

A decision was made to transfer her to a larger hospital in Columbus for a thirty-day course of radiation therapy, which hopefully would diminish her pain. However, she was in intense discomfort just being transferred to and from her bed as well as from the table in the radiation department. Each treatment meant four agonizing transfers. Her pain was out of control. There was also talk about surgery on her shoulder.

Frustrated and angry, I wondered why they couldn't just leave her alone. She was thirty miles from her family, friends, familiar doctors, and everything now was palliative (comfort measures only).

It seemed so wrong!

On Friday evening, the day after her transfer to Columbus,

her mother called me at home asking for help.

"Steph wants to come home. The doctor wants to do neck surgery, and her arm is swollen from the radiation", she told me.

I called Steph immediately.

"It's time, Carol", she said. "I don't want any more".

Her soft, gentle voice brought an anguish to my heart I cannot describe. I never wanted to hear those words, yet now she desperately needed my help, and I had to go on. She referred to Joyce's picture of Jesus, which had gone with her to Grant Hospital, and was still at her bedside. She told me that as she looked at the picture,

"I know now—there is not any more required of me but to do as He says: "Follow Me".

I assured her we would get her home as soon as possible, knowing God would make a way.

I placed a call for her local oncologist, but he was out of town. Dr. LeSar was on call for the weekend, and I asked the hospital operator to please contact him and have him call me regarding Stephanie.

He quickly returned my call. He was at the Country Club, but promised to take care of everything. I don't know whether he was at a party or a wedding reception or a business meeting, but I do know he was right where God wanted him to be.

Within an hour, he called to tell me that everything was arranged. An ambulance would bring her back to be admitted to our hospital the next day by noon. After her pain was under control, he said, she would go to her home under Hospice care. He knew she wanted to be home, and he even offered to help stay with her in order to provide twenty-four hour, round-the-clock care. I assured her mother that we would all take care of her. We could see God's hand upon this situation, and in our pain and sorrow, we all listened as God softly spoke to our hearts.

> *Follow Me. I will see to every detail. Do not lose sight of Me, for I am here.*

Pain control for Steph now meant a constant intravenous infusion of a much stronger concentration of morphine. Though she drifted in and out of consciousness for the next few days, she remained aware that her loved ones were at her bedside. As a supervisor, I could frequently take a few minutes off each day to stop in, assuring her I was there. But I left any desire of mine to spend more time with her outside her door, trusting God to help me with my sorrow.

This time was for her family now.

The last time she talked to me was on a beautiful winter day. Huge snowflakes were dropping from the sky, caressing our city with a cozy white blanket and rendering the serene quiet that only a snowfall can bring.

Steph, her voice now weak, whispered to me that Satan had been reminding her constantly that day of all the sinful things she had ever done in her life. I don't think I had ever realized the depth of evil to which the enemy will go to steal us from the Lord, but I did then — the instant she uttered those pathetic words.

My anger cannot be described. It is beyond my human ability to do so. This was not a situation that called for verbally expressing this hatred I felt toward the accuser! It was a time for blessed assurance, and as I looked at my friend so near death, my eyes caught a glimpse of the falling snow. I was reminded of a scripture we so often hear or sing, so in my own words, I repeated them to Steph:

Though your sins be as scarlet, they shall be white as snow.

> *No matter the stain of your sins, I can take it out and make you as clean as freshly fallen snow. Even if you are stained as red as crimson, I can make you white as wool!*
> (Isaiah 1:18)

Then I prayed so she could hear me and claimed that promise in the Name of Jesus. Knowing that the darkness cannot abide in the Light, I simply reminded her that the enemy had to leave as we prayed and praised the Lord.

As I stood there at her bedside, I found myself feeling so helpless and empty inside.

What more could I say?

What else did I have to give her?

What more could I do?

I knew that even to hold her hand would cause such pain, and so now, those little things that we had always encouraged others to do, seemed impossible. I was brokenhearted at my futility.

Steph had always told others that even smoothing a blanket or fluffing a pillow, if done in Jesus' Name, was 'just right'.

> *And if, as my representatives, you give even a cup of cold water to a little child, you will surely be reward-ed.*
>
> (Matthew 10:42)

But, then, as if she could read my mind and heart's desire to do something for her, Steph asked for a sip of water. After she took her tiny sip, she smiled at me, and in her soft and gentle voice said,

"Even a cup of cold water, Carol".

Thus, even in her dying, Steph went beyond her own need to meet mine, and by doing so, enabled me to do that 'one little thing' for her — and it was 'just right'.

By the next day she was not responding, though she tried to by flickering her eyelashes and moving her lips. The family was with her constantly, and I was trying to help Laura to accept the reality that Steph was dying. Everyday, when I told her about the situation, she would simply say,

"She'll wake up!"

Her thirteen-year-old mind refused to accept the truth and it was very difficult for me to help her with this.

On Thursday morning, I felt I just had to go to her room, and as soon as I was dressed, I went to the hospital, praying for just a few minutes alone with my cherished friend.

When I arrived, her aunt was with her. It was apparent that she would soon be leaving us to enter eternity. I wanted so much to have those few precious minutes alone with her, but would never have asked her aunt to leave. However, the aunt offered me to have some time alone with Steph, and I saw God's goodness toward me through her. I remembered Steph's gentle admonition to me regarding my mother's last hours.

"Talk to her and tell her how much she means to you", she had said. "Tell her what a privilege it has been to be her daughter, and to take care of her".

So this day I talked to my friend with words I never wanted to have to say. I told her how much she meant to me and what a privilege it had been to be her friend and to share two fantastic years with her. I read the comforting words of Isaiah 40 to my friend, then told her goodbye.

"I'll see you soon, Steph...I love you".

Steph's family asked me to speak at her funeral and I said I'd try. The huge room at the funeral home was filled to overflowing. Her pastor shared the scriptures she had chosen to comfort us all. Amy sang Psalm 139, Steph's favorite, and after the pastor spoke a few more words of comfort, I spoke. My attempts to sum up even the past two years of her life in a few short words were beyond my ability. To speak about the forty-five years she had lived before I met her left me woefully inadequate.

Following is a little of what I said that day:

"Once upon a time, there was a little girl named Stephanie who just loved to color pictures. Encouraged by her parents in this pursuit, she even had a special table and chair where she could sit and color page after page, her reward being a nickel a page.

This is great! she thought. And when I grow up, I'll make my living by coloring pictures.

"Well, Steph grew up and became an elementary school teacher, and as everyone knows, teachers spend a lot of time coloring, pasting, and cutting pictures for their students. And as her fellow teachers and students knew, Steph put everything she had into her teaching career.

"When illness struck her husband Gary, and shortly thereafter Stephanie too, she had to give up her job as a teacher. Yet there are very few of us who have not seen her at one time or another busily coloring her Heartwarmers, and taking time out to look up and smile at passersby. She drew them in her home, in hospitals, doctor's waiting rooms, and anywhere else she happened to be.

"The cards were not for sale, however, for she passed them out to whomever she thought needed a lift and a kind (unspoken) word. The little cards offered to 'smile at, hug, and love you all day long' and that 'they were from God'. Steph always asked God first before giving a card to anyone.

"When increased demand exceeded her ability to draw and color them, they were printed. Now found in most states, they are also printed and distributed in South Africa. These little cards, called Heartwarmers, have also been transformed into wall-hangings, dolls, sweatshirts, and cakes made by friends who wanted to please Stephanie.

"Despite grief over the loss of her husband, and weakness and pain due to her own recurrent illness, Stephanie continued to reach out to others. She encouraged many, many persons by visiting them through phone calls, but most often, by sending notes and cards regardless of her own circumstances.

"When illness deprives you of your strength, you must believe you still have a purpose. She had a long mailing list, and her death leaves a vacancy in many lives. But the legacy she has left us all is one of faith, hope, and love. Serve your Lord with gladness, in sickness and in health and tell people He loves them.

"At the Sixth Avenue Methodist Church is a group of caring people called Heartwarmers who cook and deliver soup and muffins (they warm the 'stuffins) to many people; not just to hungry people, but also lonely people, those recovering from surgery or perhaps those grieving the loss of a loved one.

"At 547 E. Walnut Street is 'The Heartwarmer Shop', a place to buy small inexpensive gifts that say, *'I care'*. Heartwarmer cards, dolls, and wall-hangings by Dolores, are also available there.

"The Circle of Hope, a local support group for those dealing with chronic and life threatening illnesses meets regularly at 151 Lake Street. This organization was founded two years ago. Steph was one of the original planners, and was an active and encouraging member.

"The Lancaster Council for the Disabled has a peer support group that provides motivational tapes which encourage its members. Steph, at one time, led this group.

"The Lancaster chapter of Hospital Christian Fellowship takes pride in being referred to as *The Heartwarmer Group* by its friends. We have been challenged to seek our potential in the Lord, and to use it all to His glory, and because of that we are forever grateful that Steph passed our way. For each one of us who have known Steph, we say,

'Thank You, Lord, for her touch on our lives'".

"Her gentle ways, her deep compassion, her uplifting love, her cute little giggle, and her abiding faith in God have deeply inspired us all. Despite our loss, we rejoice with her that she is forevermore in His presence. Our deepest sympathy is extended to her family at this time".

Lovingly submitted by one of her friends, Carol Kreici.

The pastor concluded with her favorite prayers and statements of faith: The Serenity Prayer, I Have My Mission, and the prayer of St. Francis. Lastly, he read Stephanie's poem, "If I Waited," which he was barely able to do.

Amy sang a final song from Ecclesiastes 3 titled "In His Time", and it was beautiful.

As the service closed, with Amy and I so near to the casket, an acute sense of loss pierced our hearts. We were together again, Steph, Amy, and me, one last time this side of heaven. All of our hearts were breaking.

But because of the gift of eternal life Jesus provided as He died on the cross, we knew with a certainty that we would be reunited again in that beautiful place, free of sorrow and tears.

Until then, we would trust Him for grace and the ability to follow the path laid before us, praying that our lives would reflect the Light that leads the way.

I promised myself that I would try to relay to others what I had learned from my friend in twenty-six months, 6,000 air miles, 2,500 car miles, and a lifetime of friendship.

Thank You, Lord, for my friend. I pray I can keep my promise, for You taught me so much through this wonderful person You placed in my life. I will be forever grateful.

CHAPTER EIGHTEEN

 ## DYING WITH DIGNITY

*The following is an excerpt from my
talk to the staff at the hospital where I
worked during a seminar on death, dying with dignity,
euthanasia, and the changing
definition of life in these troubling times.*

The dictionary tells us dignity means honor, stateliness. Is it possible to pass from this life to the next with dignity. With honor? Is it possible to be dying for months and retain that dignity and honor? In our profession, we try so very much to be compassionate in our care of our patients. We wish we had more time, more help, more ability, more answers. But it is not always possible, and we become discouraged or frustrated or even angry in our feeble attempts to make things better and help the 'bad' go away.

As we have discussed today, a person is comprised of three distinct parts — body, mind, and spirit. We have also talked about each area of care. We must continue to respect the whole person who has life within until that life ceases.

The sanctity of life is an issue which we must morally, ethically, and professionally deal with. It becomes more complex every day as we must decide what we believe. Life is the state of existence. Sanctity means holy or sacred. Do we see life as holy, despite the ranges of illness or pain, despite the fact that there's just not enough help to go around to allow us to do all that we want to do?

Do we see in our patient's eyes the person in there? Do we look at his or her hands and wonder how many hours and days and years of childhood fun and growing up, and perhaps parenting they have done? I believe we do, for we are a caring people.

I'd like to share a few of my personal thoughts with you. Some of you may know that in recent years I have sat at the bedside of four loved ones as they died, one after another, from cancer. Not too far from here, on two little hills in the same cemetery, are the graves of two wonderful friends. Those of you who have worked here more than seven or eight years would have probably known Charlotte Shupe, a registered nurse, mother, Brownie leader, Weight Watcher's instructor and — leukemia patient.

I remember the day she was diagnosed, and I remember too, her tears, as she tried to take it all in — the sorrow at realizing she wouldn't be wearing her nurse's uniform for perhaps quite a while, if ever, as treatment options were presented to her. The concern over how much time she'd have to be a Mom to her eight-year-old daughter, Julie, and wondering if she would live to see her daughter Cathy's children born?

She was diagnosed with a terminal illness, and yet, she continued to seek purpose in her life. If she couldn't nurse, she reasoned, then she would volunteer her services. She became enthused with her family's genealogy. She took her treatments as ordered, and endured her tests and procedures like a trooper. In her last months at Ohio State University Hospital, she visited roommates and other patients, prayed with them and told them that Jesus loved them.

Is that a dignified way to die?

I believe it is.

On the other little hill is the grave of another precious friend, whom some of you knew and loved. Her name was Stephanie Whitcraft, and if you were part of her life in any way, you know that she died here in our hospital, and that she died with dignity. She shared the love of Christ for as long as He chose to allow her to do so. While she was up and about, she had "places to go and people to see". She visited and encouraged other patients who were on chemotherapy here at our hospital, sometimes at the doctor's office or even in their homes. When not able to do that, she called or wrote cheerful notes, or sent little gifts by way of her daughters.

While a patient here in the spring before she died, she heard an elderly man moaning down the hall from her room. She went into his room and thought to herself, "Now what would Jesus do here?" She stood by his bed, stroked his arm, and said The Lord's Prayer. Then, satisfied, she left.

Later, she related this to me,

"He got quiet, Carol. Did I do anything wrong?"

"No, Steph", I said, "you did nothing wrong. Rather, you brought dignity into that room and to that man".

As she lay dying in December, her gentle spirit and smiles touched everyone's hearts here at our hospital. I do believe Steph died in an honorable way, and that each of you who cared for her needs entered into that dignity too.

About 450 miles away, on a Pennsylvania hillside, are the graves of my parents. Both died from cancer; my father, in a Pennsylvania hospital in 1980, and my mother in my home here in Ohio in 1986.

During my father's two-year illness, terminal though it was, he continued to work and have purpose. He also spent many hours just looking out the window at the beautiful Pennsylvania hills he used to roam. He dressed every day. He said 'please' and 'thank you' as we helped him. He shared his opinions with visitors on politics, deer hunting, fishing and cars, just to name a few. In his sixty years of life, he had gained much knowledge, and it was good and sound.

He chose to stay home until he was no longer able to do so. He maintained his office at work and counted on returning. His employer added to that dignity by enabling him to keep his office and phone available until he passed away. His hope was not taken away, and we were so grateful for that. He wasn't termed disposable or indispensable. Those around him gave him some honor in his dying days.

Beside his grave is my mother's, and some of you, I know, took care of her here during some very tough times. When not in the hospital, she was with my daughter and me at our home, and also went to my brother's home on weekends as long as possible. She had a complicated illness, and at times it was extremely difficult to comprehend just how long her suffering had to go on. But, again, there was dignity. She had all the skills of an R.N. daughter, enhanced by loving care from her eleven-year-old granddaughter (my daughter), other family members, friends, visiting nurses and aides. Her skin and bodily needs were cared for regularly and gently. She was given her favorite foods, and I played her favorite music when she asked me to. We tried to give her as much of 'home' as we could. We asked her opinions on things, and let her make as many decisions as possible. She remained in control of her life as much as possible. And, as she was slipping away from us in a physical sense, her physician, Dr. James LeSar, brought dignity into my home.

He sat beside her the night before she died and held her hand, calling her by her name, Ann, as if she were wide awake and talking with him, when in reality, she was comatose. For forty-five minutes, he talked with her. He talked to my mother as if she could answer him. He told her what a privilege it had been to care for her; that he had learned a lot from being her physician; how courageous she had been with all her complications, and that it soon would be over and she would be at peace.

How grateful I am to him, and I am so happy to know that this is how he cares for all his patients. He cares for them, body, mind, and spirit. He spent a lot of time over the years with both my mother and my friend, Stephanie, discussing their spiritual needs, and I will be forever grateful.

I believe it is well within our individual power to enter into a person's life and bring dignity to their dying. Do not be afraid and remember the words of my friend Stephanie's poem:

IF I WAITED

If I waited for just the right time
Just the right words
Just the right gift
I might not give at all
And then we'd both be losers.

You need something from me
And I need something from you
Today I have the extra
Tomorrow you just might
But let's not keep a score
So I venture out of my shadows,
And spot you hiding in yours
Do I pretend not to notice your presence
for lack of a proper approach?

My decision is made
I opt for some action.
You must know how much I care
Forgive me if I blunder untimely
Stammer while choosing my words
Or bear no gift at all.

At least I reached for you in the shadow
Proving how much I care.
May my little as the widow's mite
Be accepted as - just right.

CHAPTER NINETEEN

THE BRIDE

By James LeSar, M.D.

*And I saw the holy city, new Jerusalem, coming down
out of heaven from God, made ready as a bride
adorned for her husband.*
(Revelation 21:2, NASB)

1927 – THE WILSON FARM, GALION, OHIO

It was really hard for seven-year-old Dorothy to understand.
The day was like any other, but it was the day her life
changed forever. Her throat had been really sore for days. The
country family doctor arrived at the farm to take her tonsils out.
The ironing table was placed in the kitchen. Dorothy was gently
put to sleep using "drop ether" but something must have gone ter-
ribly wrong.

For at first she was asleep, and then she was hovering above
the doctor and her parents. Her parents were clinging to each
other and crying. She could see herself lying on the table with the
doctor frantically trying to revive her.

She felt no fear, but a tremendous peace enveloped her as she
heard the music - a heavenly choir of angels rejoicing in the Lord
God.

Suddenly, she was back in her body and was waking up. Her parents rejoiced that she was brought back to life. Yet, deep inside she held onto the sound of the heavenly host, a sound that she would not hear for years to come.

> *And suddenly there appeared with the angel a multitude of the heavenly host praising God, and singing, 'Glory to God in the Highest, and on earth peace among men with whom He is pleased'.*
>   (Luke 2:13)

1993 – THE LeSar FAMILY HOME, LANCASTER, OHIO

My heart was broken into the tiniest possible pieces. Dorothy, my mother, was coming home to die. Six months earlier, she called me and said the she had been ill and had gone to the local urgent care center. They told her she had some "spots" on her lungs and that she needed to get additional studies. She called me on a Monday morning and told me all about it. I tried to reassure her saying,

"Mom, don't worry. It's probably just some granulomas that are common in people from central Ohio. Send me the x-rays and I'll take a look at them."

When the x-rays arrived a few days later my heart sank. There in her chest x-rays were four or five large tumor masses.

Immediately, I called and asked her to come home so we could expedite her work-up. Within a few days, we knew that she had metastatic cancer from an unknown source, and that the specialist from the cancer hospital had recommended chemotherapy.

My mother was a strong-willed individual and she was going to do this her way. She decided that she was not going to get chemotherapy. Instead, she was going to visit all of her children and spend some quality time with them. Like many families, her children were spread out across the country and around the world. My younger brother was in New Mexico, my sister in San Francisco, and my older brother, the first-born, in Moscow, Russia. Since my older brother lived the furthest away and had a birthday coming up soon, my mother made arrangements to go to Moscow, by herself, for his birthday.

Once in Moscow, she prided herself in the fact that she got to play bridge in the American consulate. But, as expected, within a few weeks, her health deteriorated rapidly. Very quickly, my brother and I made arrangement to bring her to Ohio. When I saw her at J. F. Kennedy airport in New York, my heart was weary and heavy-laden. In six short months, she had aged twenty years. A call was sent out to her children and grandchildren, and all converged on the family home.

As the days passed, she rejoiced in all of her children and grandchildren. One of us stayed with her constantly. One night, my niece woke me up saying,

"Uncle, Jim, Grandma needs to talk to you. Come quickly!"

THE DREAM

"Mom, what is it? Are you okay? Is something wrong?" I asked quickly as I entered the room.

"No, I'm okay", she said. "I had this dream and I want you to tell me what it means. You see, I was in a church, standing at the altar in a wedding dress."

"Was Dad there?" I blurted.

"No", she said. "Now, sit there and be quiet while I tell you of this dream. As I said, I was standing at the altar and was dressed in a wedding gown. All the people in the congregation were crying. Then the music started and suddenly everyone was joyous."

"Was this the same music you heard as a child?" I asked.

"Yes it was", she answered.

"Have you ever heard that music since the time your tonsils were taken out?"

"No, I haven't", she said. "What do you think it means?"

"Mom, I think you were dreaming of your death. You are going to heaven and the fact that you heard the music again and everyone was joyous means the heavenly host awaits you. Christians can be considered the Bride of Christ".

"I think you're right", she said. "You can go back to bed now."

Within a few days, as the transition was nearing, Dorothy would say, with a look of ecstasy on her face, "It's so beautiful, I can see both sides!"

As she slipped away, I thought to myself that now she could hear 'the music' for all eternity.

It is a promise available to all of us.

PART FIVE

WHERE IS GOD IN ALL OF THIS?

CHAPTER TWENTY

COOKIES IN A
DOUGHNUT BOX

It is the fall season of 2001 and it is my favorite time of year
in Ohio. The hot, muggy days of summer have evolved into
peaceful days of brilliantly colored leaves and azure skies. There
is a certain peace within me, perhaps recalling the happy school
days of my youth. Autumn had meant getting back to school and
seeing all my friends again after the long summer hiatus. Autumn
also meant days of rain serving a thirsty ground, compacting the
leaves that had been drifting endlessly downward. I pushed to the
back of my mind memories of the older folks saying,

"Yes, fall is here, and so winter will soon be upon us".

I preferred the second version, which is that "if winter comes,
can spring be far behind?"

The fall season brought us those cool evenings, football
games were returning and 'Trick or Treating' was just around the
corner.

It was all so very innocent back then and we looked forward to
rummaging through all the old clothes and accessories with which

to create our costumes. No matter how I dressed, my brown eyes always gave me away! We lived in rural southwestern Pennsylvania, and we kids, less than a dozen of us, including my best friend Joycie, had perhaps eight or nine neighbor's homes to visit for our Halloween fun. We never even considered going anywhere else — just to our own neighbors who made it so much fun by 'guessing' our names. We would then be rewarded with big five-cent chocolate bars or homemade popcorn balls. Hershey's chocolate was my favorite, and it still is to this day. These were kinder, gentler days.

Now it is October 2001, and just a month ago, our innocence was taken away by the heinous acts of terrorists on September 11. We adults were shaken to the core, but we also were heartsick for our children, realizing they would never know such an innocent life as we had. Life here in America, and indeed the world over, was changed forever on that brilliantly beautiful autumn day as the black and heavy weight of terrorism's aftermath rained upon our cities.

Still struggling with depression and yet, trying to go on, that September day had its impact on my life, just as it had on everyone else. "Life is short," I reasoned, "so why do I remain trapped in the grip of sadness and gloom?" I fought against the strangleholds the bipolar condition and the depression had on me. I hated it, wanted free of it, wanted to be back in step with the life around me — my children, my grandchildren, my job and friends, my walk with God, and indeed, my joy in living. How long would I be separated from them all?

On one of those gorgeous October days, I arrived at my door after work, and was greeted by something I never in my wildest dreams could have expected. There was that very familiar local doughnut box at the front door. And with it, an attached note!

The last time this had happened was in the fall of 1985 and the doughnut box had been from Steph.

My first utterance was,

"This is incredible! Steph, I know you are not here, you're with Jesus!"

But I couldn't deny it. The box was there!

Tearfully, I picked it up, suddenly longing for my friend, and somewhat afraid to open the note. But I did, and amazingly, it was from Pam, the close friend I had made the year after Steph had died.

I hadn't been looking for a friend then, as I did not feel able to allow anyone back into my life. Pam was a nurse at the hospital where I worked and happened one day to walk into my little shop to buy an encouraging gift for a friend in need. As Pam and I talked that day, we found that we had much in common, and really enjoyed our little visit. Over the next few months, we became mutually involved with Hospital Christian Fellowship and with its mission of bringing Christ into our workplace. She told me I was her best friend, but I was afraid of that, and couldn't receive it. After all, I had already lost two best friends and didn't want that to ever happen again. Sadly, about a year later, our friendship was fractured after a misunderstanding and our paths seldom crossed after that. Eventually she went to work elsewhere, but dispite the distance of time and space, I tried off and on to find her, but to no avail. I was excited when, a few years later, I received an invitation to a baby shower she was having for her daughter, and that day we promised each other that we'd get together again real soon. With both of us having unlisted phone numbers however, we were unable to make contact, and so life went on.

Now, seemingly out of the blue, Pam had come to visit me. Her note said she felt she was "supposed to come and have a cup of tea, and bring something sweet to eat". Why did she stop at that particular doughnut shop, and then decide to buy cookies decorated with fall colors? I don't know, but her decision provided the title for this chapter of the book, for no other cookie bag or doughnut box would have had such a profound impact on me.

It was just right!

I knew God was in on this little treat!

Pam had written her phone number on the note, something I had tried my hardest to obtain for at least three years. Now here it was right at my own front door! I think God made sure I wasn't home so I could receive this surprise, and stand in wonderment at His Master Plan.

What's going on here? I wondered. I quickly dialed her number. Over a long telephone visit, we renewed our friendship, and eventually the subject turned to the Heartwarmers. She had never known Steph, but was well aware of the impact she'd had on so many lives and how the Heartwarmers touched others for God. I had given her some Heartwarmers back then, and it was exciting now to be sharing with her once again the thrills of living and walking with the Lord.

My spirit began to stir at the thought of a cherished friendship rekindled. So much had happened in our lives. We planned a great gab-fest to be held real soon over breakfast at a nearby restaurant so we could catch up on each other's lives. One breakfast led to another; sharing, crying, praying, and laughing a lot.

It was good, and it was healthy.

One day, she told me of how only recently she had wanted to share a scripture with her daughter as they waited in a doctor's waiting room at Ohio State University Hospital. She told me that, as she reached deep into her purse for her small pocket-sized New Testament, along came a Heartwarmer stand-up. She didn't even know she had any Heartwarmers in there and hadn't seen them for years. She became excited to be able to share this with her daughter as a special blessing from God.

Immediately, I was covered with goose bumps and couldn't wait to tell Pam that an Ohio State University Hospital waiting room is exactly where the Heartwarmers were born! Then we both had goose bumps together!

Was this a special sign from God?

We agreed it was, and, combined with her bringing the cookies in a doughnut box to my house, we knew that God was working on a plan for our lives. She told me how He had prompted her spirit that day to drive out of her way after work, and come to visit me, but that she was to stop off at the doughnut shop first. Now our prayer, mingled with the new excitement, was to find out what He wanted of us. It was thrilling, and by Christmastime, we would be filled with even more excitement, along with a better understanding of God's wishes for our lives.

In the weeks that followed, we saw more of each other, and began discussing things of a deeper spiritual nature. One day, she mentioned her 'best friend', and I asked her who that might be.

"You, of course", she said, and I was deeply affected by this.

After all these years and our lack of being able to communicate, nothing had changed. My questions regarding how to renew my 'friendship' with Jesus had just been answered!

For years, as I struggled with depression, I would ask God again and again if my relationship with Him could ever be restored, for I longed for things to be as they had been before I became sick.

Yet, in a few minutes time, He showed me that nothing had really changed. He was still my Friend, and it was the same as it always had been, just as Pam's and my friendship had been the same. Time and space hadn't altered anything. I didn't have to worry any more, for He is faithful, and our friendship would last forever.

On the day Steph died, December 11, 1986, I had written this reminder in the Bible she had given me.

> *But God is my Helper. He is a friend of mine.*
> (Psalm 54:4)

I had been assured by that scripture that despite earthly losses of those we love, we will always have our faithful Best Friend, Jesus, with us.

That verse had been a great comfort to me, as I continued on my life's walk. Now He was reminding me anew of that promise through Pam's words, and they set me free.

CHAPTER TWENTY ONE

 ## ME? WRITE A BOOK?

In June of 1988, a month after my return to Ohio from a two-week trip to Israel, I was able to join the USA Hospital Christian Fellowship Conference in Springfield, Missouri. Over the years, this organization had become an increasingly important part of my life, and by attending national and regional conferences and seminars, I had also made a lot of special friendships along the way. Though I was eagerly anticipating this conference, I was also ever-so-tired. I prayed I would be able to attend after this huge trip to Israel.

Here is an excerpt from my journal dated June 24, 1988,

"Now it is Saturday night at the HCF Conference in Springfield, Missouri. Much has happened and yet, I feel too tired to write it down. I am discouraged and confused. My spirit longing, my mind controlling.

"People are telling me to write a book. Georgia, Margaret, and Carol told me last night I should write a book about Steph! I never thought of that! Yet it sounds good! Today, Sara wrote me a note during our main speaker's talk on 'Investing in People'. Sara also needs my prayers for she, too must write about her divorce, which means dealing with remembered pain, sorrow, and feelings of rejection. Then she wrote, back to me,

"What can I do for you?"

"I kept her notes and have them in front of me as I type this today.

"I wrote her back that my request was the same as was hers to me — to pray about me writing a book about Steph as the thought had been planted in my mind the evening before. Now I needed confirmation from God. Here was her reply:

"To Carol,

"One March 1988 morning, the Lord spoke quietly to me,

"Pray for Carol, Sara. She's hurting too, in a different way." And I did.

"Later, He told me, *"Carol is going to write a book about Steph. It will be several months before she can set aside her pain and pick up her pen and do it. But she will! Would you be My silent prayer partner for her during this time, even though she is not aware of this incubating period that must be done?"*

"Oh, yes, Lord, I will, I will. Thank you for not chiding me about my pain. Instead, You've given me a reason to rise out of my pain by blessing another and to be your prayer partner."

Then, I dug out your last note to me and put it on my dressing table as a reminder — And your note often absorbed my same pain as I fell on my knees and prayed that your heart might be healed.

"God told me on the plane on the way here that this was the time to tell you. But His hand hushed my voice when I almost mentioned it to you yesterday.

"No, not yet!"

"Then, after Betty spoke this morning, God told me.

"It's time now. Tell her of our investment covenant this March, so I did.

"God revealed this to me two months ago but said,

"Carol is not far enough from her grief yet to begin. Pray for this reality".

"So I've been praying for two months. He told me You'd tell me when the time had come — and it has, dear."

I was speechless. It was as if God himself was writing an assignment on a blackboard, and it was also impossible to deny the reality of what He wanted me to do!

For the next couple of months or so, the "plans" began to develop in my mind. First, I received a title for the book and then chapter titles.

On a particularly hot and humid day, my daughter Laura and I walked to the pool so she could go swimming and cool off. Not being a swimmer, I had only to bring along a lawn chair and my sunglasses. But on this particular day, I felt I should also bring a notebook and pen.

Writing a book, I had decided, was a gigantic task. Though I had always wanted to write a book, now I was feeling more than a little overwhelmed. Yes, I had a title, and yes, I had been mulling chapter plans in my mind, but as yet, had not written a single word. This day I took my thoughts, along with paper and pen, to the pool. And there, in the heat of the day, began to bring them into reality. I didn't write much – just the book title, the chapter titles, and an outline for the chapters.

Little did I know I would not pick my pen up again for many years, and by then would need definite confirmation once again that I had not lost the opportunity to be obedient to God's direction.

An emotional breakdown, perhaps the culmination of so many losses coupled with an unknown Bipolar condition, were the culprits. Increasing tiredness, along with other classic symptoms of depression, slowly emerged, and by 1990, I found myself practically living on my couch (my cocoon, I later concluded). I had increasing difficulty doing everyday things, and my daughter eventually absorbed most of my home responsibilities.

All I knew was that I had to work enough to buy food, clothing and shelter. I communicated less with family and friends by locking the doors and not answering the phone. I found reasons to turn down most invitations to social functions, and saved what energy I had for my job and daughter.

But when I reached the point of no return, and found myself crying almost constantly, unable to evade the constant thoughts of suicide, I cried out for the help I needed. I called the hotline of a Christian Therapy Program in California, and within days, I was admitted to this facility for severe depression. This program, infused with Christian professionals in a Christ-centered milieu, was a blessing. Though I was almost totally self-isolated for the first two weeks, eventually unconditional acceptance from the staff broke through.

Despite of the unbelievable diagnosis of a Bipolar Disorder, I was determined to work within their plan of treatment as much as I could. Accepting my need for medication, its unpleasant side effects and knowing I must take these medications for the rest of my life, was news I did not relish.

But the daily doses of praise and worship, group therapy, soothing messages to Christian music, one-on-one therapy with Christian psychologists who prayed with me before each session, and the love of fellow patients, melted my heart.

I saw the other patients — fellow sojourners on the road of life — as my second family, each struggling with very difficult issues, just as I was.

Eventually, I was able to reach outside of myself and embrace others. It was just the beginning — the groundwork for my life "outside the hospital," a frightening place to be, filled with people who would not understand or accept me unconditionally, or who may include me in the typical stereotype of persons with emotional problems. I was determined to not let this stop me from trying to get well, but it was far more difficult than I expected.

The book, in the meantime, was "secreted" into the recesses of my mind. I never thought about it or talked about it. I just couldn't break through the pall of this illness.

Despite therapy, I still could find no joy in living, and intrusive, self-destructive thoughts again slyly permeated my mind. My medications were adjusted time and again in a seemingly vain attempt to bring a healthy balance to my life. This on-again-off-again pattern played havoc with my life, my emotions and my responsibilities. My denial of the diagnosis and subsequent skipping of my medicines only added to the problem.

Eventually, after many years, I decided the doctors were right, began to take my medications as directed, and have remained relatively stable ever since.

I began to long for a renewed living relationship with God, and a church to attend.

On December 11, 2001, I picked up my journal of 1987, the year Steph died. I opened it to December 11, 1987, the day she had left her earthly life and joined Jesus in heaven.

A full fourteen years had gone by!

With trepidation, I began to read — her last months, her behavior, her voiced fears, her pain, my fears — and my pain.

I read it all, through torrents of tears — fourteen years of pent-up emotion, perhaps even more, since my mother had died only a year before Stephanie in 1986.

I really think I was suffering from delayed grief, and reading the journal, despite the emotional toll, was both cathartic and therapeutic.

It put my feet on firmer soil.

I began to read the Bible again.

I talked to the Lord, fleetingly at first, but oh how I longed for my spirit to be renewed.

Eventually, I found a church and it was just right. Just what I had been longing for! And the joy that the enemy had tried to steal from me began to permeate my spirit again.

It was as though I had been anesthetized, and slowly, ever so slowly, my cells were receiving heat and light and life again.

The stage was being set by the Great Scriptwriter of our lives for the next phase of my life, and along the way, the Heartwarmers and the story of Steph, were being reborn.

He knows the business He is about!

Chapter Twenty Two

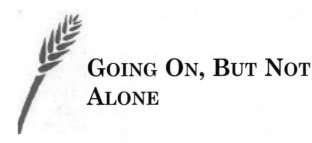

Going On, But Not Alone

After Steph died, we in the Heartwarmer group, wondered at times, 'How can we do all of this alone?' Since we believed Steph's work was God's work, we rested in the knowledge that He would take care of the future. We were so thankful that He had become a human, and that He understood all of our pain and sorrow, allowing us to grieve and mourn during our time of loss. I made a notation in my Bible on December 11, 1987 that assured me that I was not alone.

But God is my helper. He is a friend of mine.
(Psalm 54:4)

This verse continues to bring me much peace each time I read it.

Winter quickly set in and we had a cold and dreary January. Everyone hoped for an early spring thaw and for a little reprieve from winter's icy blasts. All of us in the Heartwarmer group were reassured by God's promise of eternal life, and knew we'd see our loved one again, but we missed Steph so much. We prayed for God's constant guidance for our lives.

One gray and wintry day became especially bright for me when my Aunt Boots in Connecticut sent me a flower arrangement in a rainbow mug, exactly like the one I had sent Gary and Steph after we had first met. It was as if God was saying, *"Steph's with Me, Carol. But my love goes on and on, through you and all the others"*.

Our HCF group continued to meet for the Bible Study, sharing our sorrows and joys as we always had. Amy and I had a few more speaking engagements, and Dolores continued with the shop. One evening, as we gathered together, Wanda, who had had a recent pacemaker insertion, mentioned how weak she was. She shared she could never visit cancer patients alone as she had always gone with Steph. As we discussed the many facets of Steph's ministry, we realized that in her illness and weakness she couldn't have done any one of them alone either. We reminded ourselves how the Lord had brought individuals such as ourselves to come alongside her, thus enabling her to be obedient to His wishes.

Today, Amy continues to work at our local hospital and keeps the chapel well stocked with Heartwarmer stand-ups. Wanda still heads the Heartwarmer group that she and Steph began at their church, and many cards are sent to shut-ins every month. Money received in Steph's memory has been used to provide meals for families after funerals, and the donations, given in return, have kept this ministry active for over fifteen years. Janet and I have both retired from nursing, and Dolores, Nita and Clancy have all passed on. Steph's daughter Kathi, now a mother of three, has earned her Master's Degree in teaching and works with special needs children. Tina is a busy mother of two boys, and has recently developed The Heartwarmer Shoppe*, an on-line store, making Heartwarmers available once again. Regardless of time and distance, our love for each other has never wavered.

An amazing set of circumstances, which began in the fall of 2001, brought us together again by the year's end. It all started the day I found the cookies in the doughnut box at my front door. Re-establishing my dear friendship with Pam was such a special time as we remembered our close alliance, as friends and HCF members so many years before. Talking about Steph seemed so natural and it was exciting too. I was still caught in the clutches of depression and was struggling for a release of its hold on me. When talking with Pam I felt renewed hope, and shared with her the story of how God had let me know I was to write this book.

Was it too late?

Had I passed the opportunity He had given me?

A short time after that, I received a phone call telling me that I had won a door prize at a newly-opened scrap booking shop owned by a friend. The person who called me was another friend. She was an oncology nurse and had compassionately stayed with Steph at night during her last week of life.

She told me she had recently established a non-profit organization dedicated to financially assisting cancer patients with the costs of their treatments, medications, and other necessities, such as wigs or dressings. She also said she was selling items at her shop made by cancer patients or their families to earn funds for the organization.

When I asked if she would like some of Steph's Heartwarmers to sell, she enthusiastically said, "Yes!" I immediately contacted Kathi, who told me Tina would bring some to my home the next day.

---

* www.theheartwarmershop.com

Sure enough, the next afternoon when I returned home from work, there was a box filled with Heartwarmers at my front door, along with a note from Tina. She and her sister were both thrilled to know that their Mom's Heartwarmers would be available once again in a shop in Lancaster.

Talk of the book surfaced in our conversation, and I asked them to pray specifically that God would reveal His will to me regarding writing it.

It was great to be in contact with one another again, and we decided to plan a Heartwarmer group get-together at Christmas-time.

The Christmas reunion was wonderful! After we ate, we exchanged gifts, showed pictures of our children, and told each other what had been happening in our lives since we last were together. Later that evening, over dessert, Pam shared the exciting story of how she had been able to use the solitary Heartwarmer standup she had found deep in her purse to minister to her daughter. I again asked if they each would pray that I would have clear guidance concerning writing the book. It was a wonderful evening and we all agreed that we needed to meet again soon.

I began writing in my journal again. I would advise anyone who keeps a journal to continually record all the wonderful things God is doing and has done in your life, and also to review these blessings frequently, thanking Him for His kindness each time. There is no better time to record a blessing than as soon as it happens, and there is no better time to read of those wonderful things than when life is crumbling all around you. Constantly remind yourself that He is and always has been there for you.

Though I haven't always followed my own advice, I certainly wish I had! Steph once said that keeping a 'Thank You, God!' book or journal, and reading it, trains us to see, over and over again, the little things God sends our way to help us cope over and over.

I began to feel lighter in my spirit with each passing day, and eventually came to understand that God still wanted me to write this book and to tell others of the wonderful ways in which He shows us His presence in our lives.

I had asked for, and received, confirmation through His Word, through scripture, and through confirmation from other Christians. He had provided.

One day, I told Pam how difficult I thought it would be for me to glean information from my journals to write a book. These journals were day-to-day accounts of the lives and deaths of four people I loved, and I wasn't sure I had the emotional stamina to do this alone. Pam thought for a moment, and then announced she had decided to come to my house every Saturday for three hours in order to help me go through my journals. I was so touched by this offer.

But the next Saturday, instead of being with me, she was in Anaheim, California in a sudden and unexpected role as a daughter/nurse to her own mother following surgery for cancer of the kidney. My friend, who had offered to go through this painful time with me, was now 2,500 miles away. I saw her just once in the next four months. I knew then I would have to go on alone, and hesitantly began to work on the book.

In the meantime, Aunt Boots had driven from Connecticut to Pittsburgh, Pennsylvania to visit family there. Already a victim of emphysema and coronary artery disease, she had recently also undergone chemotherapy for bladder cancer. Shortly after her arrival in Pittsburgh, she developed severe difficulty in breathing and was admitted to the local hospital. One of her favorite things to do after she began to feel better, was to hand out Heartwarmers to her roommates, their families, and her caregivers. She was a true Heartwarmer as she shared God's love with so many.

I took the last of my vacation time to visit Aunt Boots after she was discharged from the hospital to convalesce at my cousin

Susan's home. While I was there, my son Scott called from Ohio to tell me he had been hired for a new job in San Diego, California!

Unbelieving, I gulped and said something stupid like, "No kidding!"

All of my love and longing for this city, my Shangri-la, came to the forefront. Though I don't think of myself as a selfish person, I have always had to fight a gnawing sense of envy whenever anyone I knew (or didn't know, for that matter) went to San Diego.

Since 1981, I had returned to this beautiful city over and over again, every chance I had. There was nowhere else I wanted to go. At last count, I had been there thirteen times, and had, whenever possible, brought friends and relatives along. Now Scott was going to live in San Diego with his three children, and I would have to stay behind. I was thrilled for him, but sad for me.

I wanted to go too.

Since Scott is a single parent, I found myself wondering how he would be able to handle moving all his household goods, along with three children, across the country. I have to admit that my mind was generating all sorts of alternatives, such as me flying there with the kids while he drove the moving truck or, better yet, we could all drive together! I could help with the kids, I reasoned.

But ... I had no more vacation time left.

What to do?

A speck of an idea entered my mind. What if I could retire early? After discussing this with Scott, I began to pursue this possibility in earnest. After verifying with my employer that I could properly retire and obtain health insurance, I applied for Social Security.

Within four weeks, I was retired and on my way to San Diego with Scott and his children. It all happened so quickly, and yet, in such an orderly fashion. I knew God was in control.

Aside from summer clothes, and some favorite books, the

only other belongings I had packed were all my journals and notes I had collected for the book. Somehow, I had always known I would write it in California. In fact, in reviewing the journals, I have been able to see that God had been preparing me for just this season of my life for a very long time.

Before we left Ohio, I excitedly called Pam in California to tell her I'd be there soon. Her brother answered the phone only to tell me she had just left to return to Ohio, just as I was leaving! I couldn't believe it!

The trip across the United States was exciting. Our country is so beautiful and after the attacks of September 11, 2001, it seemed even more so. Every day brought new vistas, new excitement and a new appreciation for the freedom and democracy we cherish.

It took awhile for me to accept the reality of having a San Diego home address, one that was complete with graceful palm trees and lovely scented flowers everywhere. I frequently needed a reality check since we hadn't moved within sight of the city and it's harbor.

Tears fill my eyes to this day, eighteen months later, when I realize I am here where the blue of the Pacific Ocean meets the blue of San Diego's cloudless sky. Knowing that Heaven will be oh, so much more beautiful, I can't fathom what God has in store for us. The continual sun and warmth fed my spirit too, and it was good to be far away from the place that held so many sad memories. I realized it would be so much easier to write the book in this climate and these surroundings.

Scott settled into his job while the kids settled in at school. I, on the other hand, did not have to do much of anything except write. On their half-day of school each Wednesday, I would frequently take them for lunch at a nearby McDonald's, which has a play area. While they played, I worked on my book while sitting in the warm California sunshine.

One day, as we waited to purchase our food, my granddaughter,

Celena, told me that her friend, Michael, was going to be there, and that she was looking forward to playing with him outside after lunch. This meeting was possible because of the kindness my granddaughter had shown Michael at school, when some other children had been teasing him. She had seen him alone on the playground, walked over to him and made friends. Soon, the other children came back to play and the day had ended happily.

Michael had been very anxious for his mother to meet Celena. When I arrived at the table with our food at McDonald's, Celena excitedly introduced us to her friend Michael, who was with his mother. We two grownups were separated by a couple of the children at the table, and being the 'shrinking violet, bashful' type, I was going to let it go at that. But something within nagged at me to overcome my shyness and ask Michael's mother if she'd like to trade seats and sit by me. We introduced ourselves, and she told me her name was Julie.

Little did I know that she was to become my closest friend here in San Diego. We talked a bit, had lunch, and then we all went outside so the kids could play.

As Julie and I continued to learn more about each other, I mentioned I was writing a book.

"Oh, really?" she asked. "What kind of book are you writing? What is the title? What are some of your chapter titles?", she continued.

I told Julie about my friend Stephanie, the Heartwarmers, and God's directive to me fourteen years earlier to write this book. She seemed genuinely interested, and when it was time to get ready to go home, Julie made a startling announcement to me. She told me she worked as an editor and proofreader for a Christian publishing company in El Cajon, just a few minutes away from where we lived!

I was speechless!

There are millions of people living in San Diego! I was seeing the awesome touch of God on this book once again as I realized that from these millions of people, He had chosen to bring Julie into my life at this appointed time.

Meeting Julie was another of God's ways to show me I was on the right path. Though we didn't see too much of each other initially, our encounters at McDonald's soon became a ritual. By summer, as the children played together, Julie's and my friendship deepened. Sometimes we talked about my progress with the book, but mostly we just got to know each other.

As time went by, I knew that soon I would have to get deeper into my journals and confront those painful times. Thus far, I had written chapters that were of a lighter nature. I often had to read parts of the journals over and over again in order to glean the necessary information, and also to establish the proper time frames.

As I began to write the more difficult chapters, I often became sad and tearful, frequently crying as I relived those difficult years. One day, Julie said she would go through them with me, as she hated to see me do this alone. I was so grateful for her tender concern, but as I thought about her offer to me, it seemed that God reminded me of this...

"I was with you during all those years of sadness. Is it not enough that I go through them with you again as you write this book for Me?"

I realized the truth of this, and suddenly understood why I was never able to be with Pam either, regarding the journals. He had chosen for me to do it alone — but then not really alone. We are never really alone. As the words began to flow, often accompanied by the flow of my tears, He kept His promise and stayed with me through it all.

Meanwhile, Scott had a series of setbacks regarding his career and earning power in San Diego. The job he had been hired for ended a few months after we arrived, and the next job he obtained provided considerably less income. It presented a hardship that needed to be rectified as soon as possible. Returning to Ohio became an obvious necessity, and this became his goal. Neither Scott nor I had seen a spiritual connection between his move to California and the writing of this book. Yet one day, as if it were an epiphany, he told his children,

"I believe the Lord wanted Grandma to be in California to write her book. God knew she would never have retired from nursing to leave her home and move to California alone".

He told them he believed their family's move to San Diego was to 'enable Grandma to leave her comfort zone in order to fulfill the mission God had given her'.

"Now that the book is nearing completion", he continued, "I believe God will release us to return to Ohio."

This made so much sense, for as much as I had always talked about living in California, the truth was I did not have the courage to follow through on this desire. It now seemed very clear to all of us that God, respecting my fears, had brought my son and his children to come alongside me in order to bring this book to fruition. A certain peace about his job situation and the book's completion settled in, and in the days and months that followed, we reminded ourselves that God would again move in His mysterious ways to meet our needs. We tightened our belts financially and cautiously watched our expenditures.

Scott applied for jobs in San Diego and also in Ohio. During this time, the Lord honored my son's willingness to be used of Him. Before Christmas, he received an anonymous gift of $500.00 from a member of HCF who became aware of his financial struggles. Others gave him free tickets to the world famous San Diego Wild Animal Park and the San Diego Zoo.

He never once complained about the financial reverses his family endured in order to allow God to have His way in bringing me here to San Diego, and we believe God has blessed him tenfold.

The day I began writing this final chapter, Scott came home with the news he had received a promotion, and was also scheduled for an interview the next day for another job for an even larger pay increase. After he made his choice of jobs in San Diego, he received word from his past employer in Ohio that he had been selected to return to a job with them, and that the company would facilitate his return to Ohio. His earnings would be greater than when he left Ohio, just eighteen months ago, and he was being welcomed back with eagerness.

This information arrived per email on his last day of work at his current job, and just twenty-four hours after I had contacted the publisher about my completed book!

The publishing company the Lord directed me to is also an exciting glimpse of God's perfect guidance. The owners are a part of a church related Home Group I had joined some months after meeting Julie. Her husband, Gary, is the leader of this group. He and Julie are the reasons I had decided to attend since I didn't know anyone else in San Diego at the time. I did not know of this connection to the publishing company for some weeks after attending and I know that my coming to this particular group was certainly no coincidence!

God's impeccable timing leaves one speechless and filled with awesome respect for His greatness!

He never makes mistakes!

Returning to Ohio, if it is in God's plans, will be a bittersweet experience. My heart is in San Diego, and I thank Him so much for bringing me here to write this book. However, I still have my little cottage in Ohio and though my daughter Laura and her family now live in Nebraska, most of my children and grandchildren are in Ohio. At this time, I feel that is where I am to go, but I recognize the Lord may have other plans. I will go where He wants me to go.

Dear Reader,

If God has given you a task to do, He will see that it is completed. Pray for a full understanding of His mission for your life. Ask Him for discernment and confirmation from His Word and fellow Christians, and follow the road signs. He has planned each day of your life, and He will provide a 'light unto your path and a lamp unto your feet'.

One step at a time is all He asks of you.

He already knows who you will meet along the way. Keep your eyes on Him and on the goal He has given you. Keep working on that which He has given you until the last minute. Whether it is to reach millions for Him or just one, remember,

> *For a soul is far too precious to be ransomed by mere earthly wealth. There is not enough of it in all the earth for just one soul, to keep it out of hell.*
>
> (Psalm 48:8,9)

You're the greatest!

EPILOGUE

Early in the month of April 2004, after I had completed this book, I felt a great wrestling within me. We knew Scott's mission was completed, and were preparing for the move back to Ohio.

My heart was filled with sadness at the thought of leaving San Diego, even as I thanked God for the wonderful things He had done in my life during the previous year and a half.

I made a very conscious effort to think more about Ohio and what it would hold for me — my cottage, friends, church, familiar roads and stores, my doctors, and most of all, my family. I recognized that so much familiarity would feel very comfortable, and I found myself planning to resume the activities I had left behind in 2002, such as my hobbies of cake decorating, scrapbooking, and making miniatures for my dollhouse.

I won't run out of things to do, I assured myself. I'll have lots of time for my grandchildren and church activities, too, since I am now retired.

But then I remembered that almost all my friends were not retired, but still working, and I wondered how I would fill my time. Perhaps I'll write another book, I mused. As plans for my farewell became reality, I treasured each visit to my special places. At every opportunity, I took pictures of the unique tropical flowers and trees. I wanted to see the desert one more time, and the quaint mountain village of Julian, and of course, San Diego Harbor and the Coronado Bridge.

"Leaving my Shangri-la is so hard, Lord", I prayed, and I kept thinking about the mountains, the desert, the flowers, and the palm trees.

I wrote in my journal frequently, expressing my fears (and sorrow, too) for I felt so very sad about leaving California.

April 6, 2004—I busied myself with some scrap-booking while Scott had some work done on his SUV. As I worked, a new thought entered my mind. Though I had always referred to San Diego as my Shangri-la, somehow this reference to the city seemed wrong. I recognized that God had allowed me to use this term of Shangri-la for many years, but now I felt that He was saying I'd used it long enough.

So gently, yet firmly, I was sensing that my place of peace and respite was no longer a city, but a spiritual place — my special meeting place with God.

I felt this very strongly and prayed to reach that special place and hold onto it. I responded by an act of the will, and said,

"Lord, it's alright if You take away this deep longing I have to remain in San Diego. I choose to give it to You. I would like it if You would just leave me with whatever amount of my love of this city is healthy for me to keep".

I often talked to God about my feelings as I counted down the days until we would leave for Ohio.

"You know, Lord, my longing to stay here is so strong. Please let me come back. Thank You for the wonderful year and a half I have had here. Thank You for Julie, her family and my friends at the Home Group and Aubrey. The thought of being so far away from my friends makes me so sad."

He was listening.

April 11th—"Only one more weekend in San Diego, Lord".

I had begun packing my belongings, resisting the human emotion of sadness at leaving the city I had called home for twenty months. I concentrated on the positives regarding my return to Ohio. And I talked to God.

"You are my shelter and protection from the storm, Lord. My Shangri-la is where You are. Please help me to spend my remaining time here wisely. There is so much packing and cleaning to be done, and I want to spend more time with Julie, too. I would like time to go to the Home Group once more, and to talk with Mike, the publisher, again about the book. There is so much to think about, and there are still four days of driving across the country, and I just don't feel up to driving it".

With all the final preparations for the move, I realized that there wasn't going to be enough time to visit all the places I had wanted to see before we left. I was aware, however, that I wasn't feeing the urgency I had felt just a week before. Though I still had film in my camera, I felt I had taken enough pictures. It seemed O.K. if I didn't see Balboa Park or the desert one more time and I realized that, once again, the Lord had lifted the heavy sense of sadness and loss I had been feeling regarding the move away from San Diego. I felt a calmness within me and thanked Him for that, for I felt that indescribable peace, the end result, of relinquishing that which I loved once again, to the Lord.

He remains in control!

April 15th—Today, I decided to go to the monthly potluck supper of the Home Group. It would be my last time so I brought some Heartwarmers to give away, along with my camera for some parting shots of my California friends and fellow Christians.

One of the members mentioned that his wife had been meaning to call me regarding a woman who was looking for someone to share her mobile home in exchange for some help with cooking and cleaning. When I said I would be moving to Ohio in just seven days, he asked,

"Is it written in stone?"

I was dumbfounded!

Just when I had given San Diego up to God, a new door had opened! I excitedly told Julie, and she said I needed to ask for more information right away! My usual reticence took over, and I immediately responded to her,

"I can't! You do it for me...please?"

She immediately got up from the table. When she returned, a few minutes later, she had a wealth of information and suggested that, maybe, this was from God.

I brought the matter to the Lord, realizing how well He knows my heart. I believed I had truly given my longing for San Diego up to Him. I had come to realize over the past week that Shangri-la was no longer San Diego, because the sorrows and hurt I had felt in Ohio had been dealt with and put to rest by writing the book, with God in every word. He had indeed gone through it all with me once again — in that secret place of the Spirit.

I talked to the Lord about this new possibility to stay in San Diego, wondering if it was from Him, or if it was just an earthly temptation. I emailed Aubrey with this new development, and her response was simply,

"You haven't received her confirmation phone call yet, but if you do, I'd say it's of the Lord. — the same as your book!"

Later that evening, after supper, I received the phone call! It was the woman herself calling to talk to me. Her name was Barbara, and we had a very positive phone visit.

After meeting each other two days later and discussing the particulars, we agreed on the joint venture! Astounded, I found myself in her lovely mobile home, complete with an extra bedroom and bathroom, just for me! Multitudes of tropical flowers of every kind defined the perimeter of her patio, and there was even a potted palm tree!

As we talked, I learned that she was familiar with HCF and also with the Christian Therapy Program where I had been a patient so many years before. This was no coincidence!

God is full of wonderful surprises, I thought, as He continues to direct my path. He had actually pre-arranged for me to stay in San Diego. I was so unbelievably grateful!

I prayed that I would never lose sight of any of His blessings to me, and realized, too, that I must write and share with others more of these marvelous expressions of His love and faithfulness.

April 24th — We were exhausted, but on our way to Ohio at last. My car, packed with all my belongings, was safely stored in a garage belonging to one of Scott's friends. I didn't have to drive my car all the way across the country after all!

"Thank you again, Lord".

Our departure had been delayed by 24 hours because the trailer Scott had rented proved to be too small. After packing and re-packing, he eventually had to give away many items. This was difficult for him and his children, but the knowledge of a better life in Ohio gave them the ability to endure.

Our long journey had some very challenging and frightening moments but we made it and, needless to say, were very much aware of God's protection!

During the five weeks I was home, many wonderful things happened. There were opportunities to visit with loved ones and friends in Ohio, Pennsylvania and Nebraska. I was also able to accomplish the final goals for the completion of the book while I was home. A highlight was a wonderful visit with Steph's daughter Tina. She and her sister Kathi had both read the entire manuscript and gave me their written approval to proceed with the publishing.

Another goal I had was to talk with Joyce Marion, the artist whose painting of Jesus inspired the chapter, "Follow Me".

Amazingly, Joyce is now living in Lancaster, and within a mile of my home! I quickly called her, explaining my purpose, and she excitedly invited me to come to her home the very next day.

As she showed me about her lovely home, I saw it again — the beautiful portrait of Jesus., and He beckoned as before....

"FOLLOW ME"

for you never know
which will grow—
perhaps it all will."
Ecclesiastes 11:6 LB

God Bless!
Steph